BLAZER

The story of a fighting dog

By Nicholas Forster
Illustrated by Misao Fishwick

To dogs of spirit everywhere

Chapter 1

England, 1897

It was almost thirty years since Hinks had introduced 'Puss' the whiteun' into the dog pits and now on this cold gray autumn evening John Robins waited expectantly outside the 'Green Man'. The squat, muscular looking dog with the pig-like eyes sat obediently at his side. A rough hand reached down and touched the white scarred head.

"You'll show him, Blazer; you'll give him his due."

It was about 5:30 and almost dark. Word had gone around that there was to be a match round back of the 'Green Man' at twilight. Wagers had been laid, Blazer against King Nut, an all black bulldog and terrier pit bull weighing about 40 lbs. of solid muscle. Both dogs had been tried and tested in the pit; both dogs remained undefeated. In truth John Robins had kept Blazer away from Nut in order for him to gain more experience. Everyone in the village knew that a match was inevitable and whenever Robins and Jones, Nut's owner, met, the conversation invariably got around to the dogs, but never was a date fixed. But this time the taunts of Jones had finally got through.

"Right, right, happen we'll see to it," Robins had said, and the day had been fixed.

The area the dogs were to fight in was about 14' x 14' surrounded by wooden boards about 3'6" high. Rough planks were raked around the far sides in order that the spectators could view what was going on.

Bill Amner, the Landlord, had kept the pit intact as a feature of interest. The local constabulary knew of the pit but had turned a blind eye as long as the matches were not too frequent, too publicized and caused no infringement of any other laws. A few local toffs were coming down from the outlying estates to see this one—a much talked about affair—in whispered asides. Jack Furlow had done everything but put posters up on the four corners of the village.

Robins looked down at his dog and grunted, "Come on, Blazer, let's go." The short squat little canine stood up and trotted after his master. The dog knew that he was going to a 'match'; he'd done it many times before. The weeks of prior training, the extra feeds of choice cuts of beef (while his master and mistress ate lesser fare)—not that the dog realized this, but he was aware of his own ration change. He had been a pit dog for about two years; he had started 'serious' fights with high stakes at about two, and was just about in his prime. His head and face were scarred. Although

Blazer at the pit

the wounds were mostly superficial skin wounds, and the tough old head remained solidly intact, even despite the fact that only after his fourth fight he had encountered a monkey which could wield a mean dub and had suffered quite a beating before eventually securing a £40 purse for Robins; the skin never really knitted back into place but left scar tissue which added to the formidable appearance of this tough little warrior.

After the monkey, John had cashed in on Blazer's gladiatorial prowess; he had been matched against several 'good uns' and beaten most of them under the 30 minutes. He had entered an open match and wiped the floor with two old types, and chased a large mastiff-cross mongrel around the pit until the dog eventually leaped the pit wall and scattered the onlookers. He had already been down to London on two occasions and seen off the local talent killing a well favored old type that was thought unbeatable. Yes, Blazer had come up the hard way, had served his apprenticeship in the toughest arena of all. The old man thought a lot of his dog. Perhaps a contradiction in itself that if he thought so much of the dog why the hell did he shove him into the dog pit to be possibly torn to pieces?

"My dog likes a good'un, he does," John would say. "He likes to fight. If he couldn't scrap he'd die.'

White 'uns were considered chances. When they first appeared on the scene they dominated most fights against dogs of their size and then perhaps because of the out-crossing with Dalmatians or dubious dogs lacking the fighting stamina and gameness of the pit dogs the occasional batch would let the side down badly. But usually when a good one turned up it was a good one. John's dog had the muscular strength, the powerful shoulders, and the long large head with the piggy almond shaped eyes, a decided advantage in the pit enabling the dog to have a comprehensive vision of what was going on behind him. The jaws lacked the massiveness of the regular old type but were nevertheless equally adept at holding on. It didn't really matter what a dog looked like or how big he was; the most important feature was the dog's gameness, his desire to keep going no matter whether he was winning or losing, to keep fighting regardless of pain or conditions, to keep trying to win. In the past, in the earlier days of bull baiting, it was not unknown, after a dog had been put to stud, for him to display the ultimate in tenacity by being severed in half while still clinging to a bull. The price of the pups usually increased after this display—although there was still a chance that the pups might not inherit their progenitor's courage.

Such practice hardly did much for the furtherance of the 'sport' and bull baiting eventually was made illegal. The sheer size of the area needed, and the conditions required, together with the problem of concealing a bull, made any illegal meetings hardly viable. With dog fighting it was much easier to disperse a crowd and lose a few dogs in the melée. It was by crossing these bulldogs with the terrier types that the bull and terrier dog—a dog used for fighting other dogs, smaller and more agile than the 80 or 90 lb. bulldog—developed. Gradually the dog became known as the bull terrier, a courageous fearless dog that would have a go at anything. Then Hinks, interested in bull terriers, took a fancy to the white dogs that occasionally cropped up at meetings by crossing this type with the old English white terrier and another breed thought possibly to be a Dalmatian and developed a slightly larger dog which bred true to form and became very fashionable. Puss, his first English Bull terrier, proved herself in the pit as well as the show ring, and won £5 for Hinks by beating one of the old type in several minutes. This established the breed in dog fighting circles and although the odd specimen didn't come up to scratch, generally the breed lacked none of the gameness of his ancestors. It can also be said that the odd cur turned up even from the most tried and proven stock of the old type.

Blazer trotted into the pit. Several people had already seated themselves on the raked planks, the 'audience' ranged from several well dressed gentry to a few urchins, their noses running and faces alive with interest. The back of the inn smelled of tobacco fumes and alcohol. There hadn't been any previous meetings for at least a month, although the air still had a strong animal-like flavor.

A round faced man with a long black overcoat sat watching in the third tier. His name was Ian Campbell, an American here to conduct some business with one of the local mills, who had an interest in the 'Pits' as this sport was flourishing in America and good dogs were worth a lot of money. He had been to a couple of venues while he had been in England on the invitation of one of the mill owners. Although these matches were filled with spectators and one would at first glance think tickets were issued at the door, it was arranged purely by word of mouth and under a strict cloak of secrecy, although John Robins felt at this particular moment that any second now a fanfare would start up and a ringmaster step in.

"There's a lot of folk here," John said. "Aye, it's a good match."

"One that's been talked of for some time," replied Bill the Landlord.

"Ay, Blazer'll show him."

"Well, looks like his chance is just coming in."

Jones was leading a small solid black chunky little animal into the pit. Blazer caught sight of the other dog and stiffened, staring fixedly across at the other animal.

Joe Black, a local, stepped into the pit and kicked the sawdust more evenly over the floor.

"All right, bring in the wash tubs."

Two men entered from the exit to the tavern carrying wooden tubs of warm water. Joe went over to each and smelled each bucket.

"Which bucket, Jones?"

"I'll have the left."

The bucket was handed to Jones and he went over to Robins' dog, leaving Nut with his handler. Each owner had a handler and Joe Black was refereeing. Joe said, "Okay, the dogs were both weighed this afternoon. Nut being a pound heavier. All right, start washing him."

Jones approached Blazer with the bucket of water. "All right boy, let's have you, come on then." Blazer remained motionless while Jones rubbed the water over the dog's head and body, Joe keeping an eye on the whole procedure.

"There's a good 'un," Jones said as he finished washing Blazer. Blazer wagged his tail a couple of times and returned to his vigil.

"Right. Let's go to it," Robins said as he picked up his bucket and went over to Nut. The solid little dog wagged his tail as the men approached. He knew the procedure well and was gamely waiting for the first scratch. Robins ran his hands over the well-muscled body noticing the scarred flank and chewed ear. The broad powerful head which enabled a dog of this type to clamp onto some unfortunate creature and prove virtually impossible to remove. He wondered if Blazer could win. He didn't doubt his own dog's courage, but this seemed a very physically powerful dog in prime condition. But there again Blazer had sorted out equally tough looking dogs in the past. Don't fall for that appearance line, he told himself, don't mean ought what dog looks like, it's what he fights like that counts.

When he had originally entered the room he had felt decidedly chilled, but now under the oil light and with the mounting numbers of spectators he felt almost hot.

" 'Ave you done?" Joe said.

"Aye, he's okay by me," John replied, and patted the chewed ear of Blazer's adversary.

"Right, let's have a look at Nut." Joe examined each dog carefully looking for any 'aids' that could enable a dog to get an unfair advantage. He then examined Blazer, his coat still wet from where Jones had washed him. It was not unknown for owners to 'treat' their dogs' coats prior to a match, the 'treatment' eventually affecting the other dog's performance.

Blazer vs. *Nut*

"Right. Take 'em to corners and dry 'em off."

A scratch line was drawn in the sawdust. Blazer was still staring fixedly at Nut who was responding to the visual challenge. Each dog knew and was eager to go. The spectators began to settle down to the business of watching. Bill Amner was always keen to 'entertain 'round back' as he called it, as it always brought in a lot of thirsty punters. Food and drink was supplied before and during the 'entertainment.' A coin was tossed. John won the call.

"Face yer dogs." The two handlers turned the dogs toward each other from their perspective corners.

"Okay. Release the white 'un."

Blazer shot across the pit like a bullet and Nut braced himself for the impact as the handler released him. Both dogs met head on growling and snarling. The spectators shouted and cheered. John yelled encouragement at Blazer.

"Get in, Blaze, take his cheek."

Blazer had secured a firm hold on Nut's shoulder, Nut was trying to turn and secure a grip on Blazer. Blazer pushed, his strong hindlegs taut like steel against Nut's struggling fury. Nut was slammed against the side of the pit. A cloud of dust gradually settled as the dogs turned and wrestled to the other side. John watched. He knew the fight was far from over, although Blazer had a grip. It wasn't a finishing one. He had seen him go for the throat but Nut, being the experienced dog he was, had ignored the feint and turned his shoulder. Blazer was trying to secure a firmer grip; Nut felt the jaws slacken for an instant and pulled simultaneously. The black dog struggled loose and faced the white snarling fury. Both dogs now wrestled and shoved to 'get in.'

"Come on, Blaze, take him."

"He'll see yours off now, Robins," Jones remarked.

"Like 'ell he will."

Joe Black danced nimbly around the pit as the dogs snarled and wrestled for an opening. Blazer went down as Nut leaped onto the top position. Nut's jaws closed firmly 'round Blazer's leg as Blazer clamped onto the already chewed ear. The steel jaws tightened on the strong white leg, but if he felt any pain he didn't manifest it. His coat was covered in saliva and flecked with blood and sawdust and he was still intent on securing a firmer grip.

The crowd murmured its approval as the two dogs kicked the sawdust up, obviously two game fighters. The American had sat stony-faced throughout, although he had been impressed, stood up and crossed over to a swarthy man of about thirty-six, with bad teeth, wearing a dirty scarf and a cloth cap. He had been busy taking wagers prior to the fight.

"Am I too late for a bet?"

"No sir, you've still time. Who's yer boy?"

"I'll have five on the black."

"Shillings, sir?"

"No, pounds."

"Ay, sir—ay."

Reece took his bet. Must be a toff, he thought although he didn't talk like one.

The American went back to his seat. Meanwhile the two dogs were still going hammer and tongs in the confines of the pit. Blazer was still underneath with Nut over him; Blazer was working away as best he could at the lower jaw of Nut, showing no signs of turning. Finally, Blazer got the cheek of Nut and pulled with all his strength; Nut's head went with the tug and he toppled over, his jaws still firmly round Blazer's foreleg. Neither dog could get to it s feet so they both remained in a tangled knot, neither moving except to reinforce their grip.

Joe came over. "Scratch the dogs," he yelled.

Both Jones and Robins went to their dogs. Jones took a hold of Nut by the scruff of his neck and reached under to grip his windpipe. Robins held Blazer in the same grip, each handler squeezed the windpipe of their dog simultaneously. After about a minute both dogs released their hold, panting and gasping for breath. Jones picked up Blazer and took him back to his corner. His leg was chewed although the bone wasn't broken.

"Face yer dogs," Joe called from the scratch line.

This time it was Nut's turn to scratch first. No sooner had he been released than he shot across the pit, slamming into Blazer and pinning him against the slats. Both dogs shoved and pushed, using their shoulders and mouthing each other. Nut could sense that Blazer's leg was a weak spot and went in low to try and take a grip. Blazer crouched lower and presented his jaws, pushing forward at the same time. Again Nut turned his shoulder and pushed; the sawdust slewed up as his strong back legs locked solid. This time he tried for Blazer's other leg. Blazer again avoided the steel jaws and turned his shoulder.

"Take up yer dogs," Joe shouted.

"He didn't turn," Robins objected.

The crowd shouted, "Take 'em up."

Both handlers once again stepped in and took up their dogs. If a dog turns away or shows any signs of wanting to run then he is immediately taken up and scratched. If he fails to cross the scratch line or shows signs of hesitating then the other dog is the winner. The dogs were taken back to their corners. Blazer was showing the worst signs, although still very much in the fight. The 'old type' had a slimey appearance and steam was rising off his muscled body, his ear and jaw were bleeding where Blazer had gripped him.

"Let 'em go."

John released Blazer. "Go in Blaze, keep at him." Blazer waddled across the pit and went straight in, showing every inch his gameness.

The crowd applauded and the American nodded approvingly. Fifty minutes later the dogs, more tired and blood-covered, were still snarling and engrossed in their objective to be top dog. Blazer had managed to keep his chewed leg out of the way of Nut's powerful jaws, but had been gripped firmly by the shoulder just managing to tear himself loose before Nut secured a tighter grip dangerously near his throat.

The battle was taking its toll of both dogs' stamina. They had slowed down considerably and the crowd had now fallen silent as the two fighters scratched once more.

Blazer again raced across the pit. Nut lowered his head and took the dog's impact on his thick skull. Blazer spun round and round and his flank slammed into Nut's head. The blow took Nut off balance and Blazer seized his chance as the dog crashed against the wall. He turned and caught the offered throat securing a powerful grip just above the heaving chest.

The American stood up and then sat down again. Jones clenched his teeth as he watched Nut's jaws, slashing the air, his eyes strangely staring and the whites clearly discernible as he strained against the vise-like grip. Blazer settled down; he knew that all he had to do was just hang on. Jones shuffled from one foot to the other.

The crowd began to react, sensing that it was the beginning of the end for the black one.

"Call 'em off, take 'im out."

Joe looked toward Jones.

"Well."

"All right, all right."

The crowd echoed their approval as Robins, a smug grin on his face took hold of Blazer's throat.

"All right Blaze, let's call it a day."

The dogs were separated after Robins eventually pulled Blazer off, the easiest way to get a dog to release its grip. The dogs were quickly faced away from each other and held in their respective corners.

"Do you want another scratch, Jones?"

"No, I reckon he's still there," Jones told Black.

Nut, although the loser, was still raring to go and have another crack at Blazer.

"You got a good'un there, Jones," Robins remarked. "A real good'un."

The crowd applauded and cheered as the dogs were taken out of the ring. It had been a good match. The American, although five pounds poorer, smiled as he watched Blazer trot out of the ring, his foreleg badly bitten and bleeding, with several deep gashes along his flank, but still perky with a jaunty gait.

"That's a good dog you've got there, sir," he said to Robins. "Do you want to sell him?"

The bargaining had gone on for some time and although Robins had at first refused to sell, the price of £600 had eventually won him 'round. "Besides," he thought, "I can use one of Blazer's pups." Blazer had recently enjoyed an afternoon's introduction to Fred Turbins' bitch, a similar white sort with a good reputation in the pit. Robins was to have first chance at the litter. "If one of them don't show true to form I'll be right surprised," he thought, "perhaps even better."

"Okay, then the dog's yours. He'll need to rest up for a while if you intend to use him for what he's bred for."

"Don't worry, he'll rest and get the best of food and attention. He'll need it for what I have in mind for him."

"You ain't from these parts," Robins commented."No, I'm from America."

"That a fact—are you going back there?" Robins enquired.

"Yes, as soon as possible. I've finished my business here. I just wanted to wait a couple of days to clear a few things."

"Oh, aye." Robins took the money and began counting it.

Most of the people who had filled the seats had dispersed, a few had come over to Robins to offer him congratulations and to thank him for fattening their purses. Robins' purse too was considerably fatter, and he could live quite comfortably for about six months on what Blazer had just earned him, plus now he could virtually retire on this £600.

"You show 'em, Blazer," was his only comment as he watched Campbell lead the tough little whitun away limping slightly on his torn leg.

Blazer looked 'round to see if Robins was following, but yielded to the strong pressure of the rope tied around his neck. His wounds were just beginning to be painful and his blood was no longer racing through his body.

"Come on, Blazer," Campbell soothed, "Let's go and patch you up and give you some grub. You'll have plenty of time for resting once we get aboard the ship."

>>>>OXXXXOXXXXOXXXX

The journey across the Atlantic had been smooth, the weather had remained reasonably calm although very cold. Blazer's wounds, with the aid of good food and plenty of exercise around the decks, inhaling good clear sea air had healed almost to just scar tissue and his leg was as good as new. In the time Campbell had spent with Blazer he had grown very fond of the animal, treating him with affection and admiration. He had also been thinking how he was going to train this gladiator into peak perfection. The dog's weight had gone up from 40 lbs. to about 51 lbs. in the last few weeks, voraciously working down all the food that Campbell had put before him. He was not concerned that the dog had put on weight; besides he needed protein to heal his scars and build the muscle that Campbell intended to put on him. When eventually they arrived in America it was a heavier and healthier Blazer that waddled down the gangplank.

The docks were full of people milling and jostling, barrows trundled to and fro' along the cobble stones and the smell of fish hung in the air.

Campbell, after disembarking, went to a nearby stall and waited.

"Ian, Ian," a well dressed woman wearing a wine colored lace-trimmed dress and a cape and bonnet, was waving her parasol at Campbell.

She rushed forward to Campbell and threw her arms around him. Blazer looked up and wagging his tail jumped up at the couple.

"Ian, I've missed you so much, I've only just got your letter. Tell me everything. How was it? How long did it take you? Did you see—Ian, what on earth is that?

Fiona Campbell had broken from her embrace and was looking at the porcine animal jumping up at her.

"Now, now, my dear, one question at a time—and **that** is a dog. Come, where's our carriage? It's really good to see you. Come on, Blazer."

The three of them walked towards a carriage that was attended by a stocky Irishman.

"Sean, good to see you." Campbell shook the man warmly by the hand. "How are you?"

"Fine, sir, fine, sir, it's good to be seeing yourself. Well, well now look ee here, a fighting dog you have with you. He's not the regular type." He stooped down and patted Blazer's head. Blazer wagged his tail and jumped up bringing his tough scarred head next to O'Hara's.

Blazer lands in America

"Now let's be having a look at you. There's a good boy." Blazer snorted and shuffled as the Irishman looked him over.

"Is this the one you've bought for February, sir?"

"It is Sean, it is."

"Oh, come darling, I haven't seen you for nearly six months and all you can talk about is dogs," said Mrs. Campbell. "Let's go back to the house, have some refreshment and you can tell me all about your journey."

"All right, my dear, I'm sorry. Sean, tether Blazer behind the buggy; some road work will do him good; then give him some food and drink when we get back to the estate and we'll start him off."

Sean took Blazer, tethered him to the buggy and they set off from the bustling dock area through the town and into the countryside, Blazer straining and barking at every horse that trotted by. The clouds overhead hung gray and heavy as the horse and buggy, the little white dog trotting close behind, made its way to the Campbells' home.

The estate was about five miles from the city area and covered about two thousand acres of rich pastureland where sheep grazed. Blazer had trotted easily behind the buggy, although if he had been free he would have been among the sheep at the first opportunity. Campbell was quite wealthy. His parents had come from Scotland in the mid-1800's and had raised sheep. The farm had gone from strength to strength and Campbell now had business ties throughout America, Scotland and Northern England. It was while on one of his business trips that he had first encountered the pit dogs of England. In America, dog fighting was becoming more popular, although it was frowned upon by the law. The prime source of good fighting stock came from British pits and of course the Irish dogs had a good reputation as 'punchers'—dogs that hit hard and tenaciously. Sean had been among the few who had introduced good Irish lineage into the American Pit dog that had emerged. He had heard of the white sort and hadn't taken much notice of them, but always judged a dog after he'd seen it in action rather than scorn it for its first appearance.

"Sure, it looks like a pig," he said to Campbell as they walked up the tree-lined drive to the stables.

"Yes, but the similarity ends there. Keep him tethered, Sean, for the Lord's sake; if he got loose then God alone knows what would happen to our stock. I'll see you tomorrow. Don't forget to feed him, only the best, mind you, only the best." Campbell turned and walked away toward the house, his wife already having gone in.

"All right, all right, I'll be seeing to you, Red as soon as I've sorted out this piglet." Sean went around the back of the house to the storage cupboard and returned with a large piece of beef.

"This ought to do yer." Blazer wagged his tail and snorted, the peculiar type of grunting sound that he made when he was pleased. Sean took an axe and a sharp knife, hacked a piece of meat off and cut it into several chunks. He put these into a bowl and set it down before Blazer in the barn.

"We'll have to get you a collar, matey, so I've got something to take hold of you with. Get that down yer. I've got things to do. Be seeing yer later—sleep well, me old boy; yer'll be a needin' it." Sean closed the barn door and went over to attend to the horse.

Chapter 2

In Boston about this time, as in many places in America, dog fighting was very popular and one of the current favorites was the Boston terrier, a cross bulldog and terrier similar to the bulldog type of the British pits, but with a rounder head and more bulldog appearance. A tough little dog unlike his modern counterpart, which has been bred out of recognition, emphasis being made on the undershot jaw and large ears, distinct disadvantages in the pit. Many contests took place in the dock area, or warehouses rented for the evening, or behind a market square. As in England the fights were well attended and a lot of money changed hands.

Campbell had not intentionally become involved in the dog pits but had always admired the tenacious courage of the pit dogs, their gameness, stamina and strength. Probably it was easier for him to stand at the edge of the pit and watch his dogs go through the motions demonstrating their prowess which perhaps was lacking in 98% of the spectators. Probably if any of the human beings were faced with the same ordeal it is more than likely that they would manifest the attitude that they so despised in a dog—that of total fear of being injured.

However, this was not the case of Sean. He was a tough fighting Irishman who even now would take on all comers if the purse was right, and at 45 he could still lay out many a younger man. He was one of the old school. His father had fought dogs in Ireland and he himself had brought two good stock dogs out with him that had paid his fare and sustained him for two months. After that he had taken to prize fighting and it was here that he met Campbell. Campbell was in need of a good hand and one who knew about dogs, for he had unwittingly purchased one of Sean's dogs through an agent, and the dog, although doing well, was not at his best.

"He needs a good handler," had been the advice of one of his hands and Campbell had set out to find one. His wife considered the whole thing barbaric and for the 'lower types' and could not understand her husband's interest in the nasty affairs. As far as she was concerned, Blazer was an ugly little creature that should be chained up and used solely as a guard dog.

"You don't understand, my dear. If he doesn't scrap, then he's unhappy."

"I can hardly believe that. How can you say he's happy when he's being bitten and attacked and suffering?" Although having seen Blazer with his jaunty gait, scarred head and twinkle in his eye she was almost inclined to believe her husband.

The following day a horse and buggy drew up outside the house; a tall well-dressed man stepped down from the carriage.

"Campbell, good to see you."

"Richards. How are you?"

The man Campbell addressed was a well-to-do landowner, Frederick Richards, having a spread about three miles south. He was highly respected in the town and a good friend of Campbell's.

"Have a good trip?"

"Fine, come in and have some tea or something; it's too cold to talk out here."

"Fine, fine, although I hear you brought a companion back with you."

"News travels fast—you want to see him."

The two men exchanged pleasantries as they walked towards the barn.

"Did you see him work?"

"I did; I even put money on the other dog."

"What on earth for?"

"Just in case I was wrong."

"You obviously weren't."

"No, he's still a bit cut, although virtually healed."

In the barn as he heard the sound of footfalls and voices, Blazer looked up from his curled position. He was already standing at the barn door, wagging his tail.

"So this is he," Richards remarked. "This is the one that's going to win for you, is it?"

"Well, I know that if he doesn't, it won't be for lack of trying. He's a dog of the Hinks variety." Campbell explained, giving Richards the benefit of the information he had learned while in England. "A few of the gentry have been showing this sort."

"Show 'em and they get soft," put in Richards.

"I agree, but he's no soft one."

The dog they both admired bore little resemblance to the bull terrier of today. He had no 'down-face' and although he was chunky gave the impression of being lithe and muscular. His ears were also quite small and not pricked, but the eyes were pig-like and triangular.

The purpose for which Campbell had brought Blazer was to win a wager against a dog that had been unbeatable for the last two years—a tough bulldog type American pit dog that had defeated every dog it had met. Brady, the dog's owner, had sent out a challenge to anybody that the dog would take all comers and all breeds. Because of the dog's prowess, the size of the purses increased and Brady was making money.

Campbell had already set one of O'Hara's dogs against the American and had lost, the dog eventually dying from its wounds. The taunting of Brady and the arrogance of his manner had riled Campbell to the extent of his urge to put Brady's dog in its place.

"So you reckon this one can take Brady's?" Richards commented as he fondled Blazer's head. "Did you hear that there's to be some sport Friday fortnight at Henessees'?"

"How many matches?"

"Two, I think and believe one of the trappers has got a timber wolf he's going to bring for an opener."

Campbell thought for a minute. "Perhaps I ought to take Blazer for some exercise."

"What's his condition?" Richards asked as he ran his hand over the dog's shoulders and flanks. "He still seems a little overweight; that shouldn't be too much of a problem. I'd give him another month."

"Maybe," Campbell said, "I'll let Sean decide."

Blazer was now getting quite boisterous and had taken hold of Richards' glove.

"Hey, steady, steady."

"I wouldn't pull against him or you won't have any fingers left in your gloves." Campbell disentangled the glove from Blazer by diverting his attention to an old rope that was lying in the barn. When Blazer released the glove in favor of the rope, Campbell returned it to Richards.

"Come over to the house and we'll have a brandy. I'm sure Fiona would be delighted to see you and I'll tell about my trip."

"Things aren't going too well in South Africa, I hear."

The two men left the barn and crossed over to the house. Sean passed them as they walked from the barn.

"How are you, sir, Mr. Richards?"

"I'm fine thanks, Sean. I see you've got another challenge to Brady."

"Aye, sir, and this one's going to beat three kinds of hell out a that mangy cur, with respect, sir."

"Mr. Campbell seems to think so, eh, Campbell?"

"I do indeed. Oh Sean, take Blazer out this evening for a spot of exercise and then give him a go on the harness."

"Aye, sir."

The harness was a leather restraining device fitted around the dog's body with varying weights attached to the end. It was usually situated on a slope. An inducement to make the dog pit his strength against the weight was made, the bait being kept just out of reach of the dogs jaws. If the dog pulled too easily then more weight was added. To strengthen the dog's jaw muscles the animal was encouraged to take hold of a stick or leather and pull against it, being lifted from the ground for greater lengths of time, starting with a few seconds and then eventually just letting the dog hang up by his jaws for several minutes knowing that he'd just hang there without letting go. Also the dog was encouraged to jump for tidbits. The training of the dogs was done by harnessing and directing the dog's strength and energy along their natural lines.

It has been said that, pound for pound, the pit dogs were the strongest animals alive. They certainly were the most game. Varying methods were used to train dogs. One method which Sean employed to strengthen the dog's hind legs was to encourage the dog to retrieve a stick and then to throw the stick downhill, the dog then fetching it by climbing the hill, a slightly heavier stick being substituted each time, until the dog showed signs of fatigue. The sticks were made beforehand and suitably weighted, thus eventually making the dog climb the hill with a considerable weight, motivated purely by his own desire to meet the challenge and enjoy the game.

Later that afternoon after Sean had completed his daily chores he went into the barn and took a rope hanging from one of the timbered walls.

"Come on, Blazer, we'll go for a stroll and give you some exercise."

They left the barn and made their way to a wooded area about half a mile from the house. Sean looked around.

"I see no reason why you shouldn't have a little freedom." He slipped the rope from Blazer's neck. "Go on boy, go on." Blazer shook himself and took to the serious business of sniffing the ground, examining clumps of grass here and upturned soil there. He marked a tree and trotted off into the woods ahead of Sean. He stopped occasionally to look back to see if Sean was following.

"I'm here, matey; go on, go on with yer."

They had been walking for about half an hour when suddenly Blazer stood stock-still on the path. Sean was about fifty yards behind him.

"What is it, Blazer?" What had brought Blazer to a sudden stop was the sight of a sheepdog belonging to Tom Arnot, standing in the middle of the track. "If he gets hold o' that it's going to cost me money," thought Sean.

Once Blazer had made up his mind, there was absolutely nothing in the world that could stop him. As with most breeds once they are in full flight they are deaf to command. Being a pit dog, the sight of another dog loose was the signal to attack and Blazer did just that. His hackles went up and he ran forward totally ignoring the abuse and the stick that was hurled at him.

"You son of a ..." Sean wished that the dog was obedient. They had a stubborn streak that couldn't be beaten out but as in their training had to be

Blazer goes after Bess the sheepdog

twisted so as the dog thought he was doing what he wanted.

The sheepdog, sensing that Blazer was rushing to the attack, took off within a few yards of Blazer's jaws. The two dogs disappeared into the woods. Sean knew it was no good trying to call the dog so he resignedly trotted down the path in the general direction of where he'd seen them last.

Bull terriers, although not the fastest creatures on four legs, have ample speed in the initial rush to catch most things they chase. Perhaps because the sheepdog had waited too long before it took flight, or the restrictions of the woodland or whatever, but Blazer was alongside it in no time. Had they both started off at the same time and the distance over a mile or even five hundred yards, the sheepdog would have left Blazer standing, but in this case and these circumstances, the sheepdog halted about two yards in front of Blazer and crouched down. Blazer went straight over the top of the other dog crashing into some undergrowth, turning instantly while still entangled. What he saw when he faced the dog was not a snarling adversary with lips drawn back ready to fight, or even a clean pair of heels, but a submissive dog on its stomach wagging its tail with its head outstretched. Blazer was faced with two instincts, the instinct to leap on the dog and finish it, the one which had been bred in him or the instinct to recognize submission and leave it at that. He stopped his attack and stood watching the dog, moved slowly forward and eventually stood over the sheepdog his head and jaws close to the dog's throat. An ominous growl rumbled in his throat. The sheepdog remained motionless except for the tail wagging. The two dogs

Blazer stands over the submissive Bess

stayed in this position for some time. Then Blazer stiff-leggedly stepped back keeping rigid and primed for attack if the need should arise. His head gradually came closer to the hindquarters of the other dog and his nose probed in order to discern his next move. His tension eased a little, the stiffened white hair on his neck gradually lowered and he stepped off the prostrate animal and urinated up against a nearby tree. The sheepdog stood up slowly, went over to the tree, sniffed it and then cautiously came over to Blazer wagging her tail and keeping her head low. Blazer kicked the soil with his hind legs and relaxed.

The sheepdog was a bitch. Although not in season her strong scent and passive attitude had saved her life. The bitch was wagging her tail furiously now; the danger over and the relationship established, she began to bark in Blazer's ear and nipped it playfully. Blazer turned down the path and trotted off, the bitch shouldering him as he walked, trying to get a playful response. Suddenly Blazer tucked his tail between his legs and ran round and round kicking up the leaves spinning in one spot and then racing off again. The bitch pursued him and it was this sight that met Sean as he came into the clearing where the dogs were. Blazer came racing toward him with the bitch in hot pursuit, the pair of them nearly knocking him over as they rushed past.

"Well oi'll be, I thought you was a gonner," he muttered to himself as he watched the dogs racing round.

"That'll give you a little bit of exercise." Sean knew that two dogs when free usually exercise far longer and far better than one. But the problem

with the pit dogs was that they didn't usually toler-
ate other dogs, although Sean had known of one in
Ireland a regular warrior that had been brought up
with a small mongrel, both dogs being of the same
sex. The mongrel was the older of the two and had
put the pit dog in 'his place' several times. The pit
dog could quite easily have killed the mongrel in
seconds, but tolerated the rebuffs it got for its per-
sistent ear chewing and constant playfulness with
the little dog. No other dog could have come near
it.

"Come on, Blazer, we'd best be getting back, I've
got to give you a go on the harness and besides
I've got work to do." Sean turned around and began the walk back. Blazer trotted ahead with the
bitch in pursuit.

"Come on, let's put this rope on 'cos we're getting near to the farm and I don't trust you one inch
with them chickens. Well, well, what have we here
then?"

A small girl of ten years wearing a long yellow
dress and black boots, carrying a stick, was coming
towards them. She caught sight of the sheepdog
and called out.

"Bess, Bess, you naughty dog, where have you
been?"

The sheepdog on hearing the little girl's voice
raced up the path toward her. Blazer who had just
avoided being put on the leash, rushed after Bess;
the two dogs jumped up at the little girl, wagging
their tails. The weight of Blazer caught the girl off
balance and she sat down with a thud. Blazer immediately covered her face with his wet tongue,
snuffling in her ear. The little girl, being used to

Mary meets Blazer for the first time

dogs, laughed out loud as the dogs licked her.

"Looks like you've got a couple of pals, Mary Arnot. What are you doing out here?"

"I was looking for Bess, Mr. O'Hara. Daddy says she's a useless good-for-nothing and hopes she's gone for good."

"Well it's true, she's not one of your daddy's best dogs but she has a few saving graces."

"Saving graces?" the little girl replied.

"Well you know—good points."

"Oh yes, Mr. O'Hara, she's the best dog in the world, and she likes your dog too."

"Mr. Campbell's dog."

"He's a funny shape, ain't he; what's his name?"

"Blazer."

"Has he hurt his face?"

"No that's how he should be."

"Oh, he's friendly, isn't he?"

"He certainly is; now come on, I'll walk back with you to your place; it's too cold and besides it'll be getting dark soon."

Sean, the little girl, and the two dogs walked back in the direction of Arnot's place.

"Perhaps yer daddy'll lend me a horse 'cos I'm a little behind time as it is."

"Oh, I'm sure, Mr. O'Hara," the little girl replied and took Sean's gnarled hand in hers. "Come on, let's run."

Tom Arnot willingly lent Sean a horse, although his problems were far from over when he mounted. Blazer had always disliked horses and had to be kept tied up while the horse had been saddled. There was no way that Sean could have had the

40

dog on a leash and been on horseback at the same time.

Eventually he had ridden a few yards out of the farm gate, Arnot restraining Blazer and then kicking the horse's flanks into a gallop, shouting to Arnot to release the dog. Blazer flew like a bolt from heaven upon release.

The horse raced away into the fading light. The only way of getting back to the estate on horseback with the dog was to outrun him. The horse thundered along the track—Sean had always fancied himself as a jockey, although he knew he was too heavy, and imagined as he felt the great powerful animal beneath him and the wind racing through his hair that he was on the final lap of a race on which his fortune was to be made.

Blazer came on behind, the gap gradually closing between dog and horse.

"Come on, yer mangy cur," Sean cried out. Blazer began to bark as he drew close to the horse. It was a good hard ride back to the estate and the horse was tired as they saw the light of the big house. Sean leaped off the horse and caught Blazer by his makeshift collar just as he was about to snap at the horse.

"Come 'ere, you 'orrible 'ound." He gripped the dog's collar and took hold of the reins of the horse, leading the animals into the driveway in a crouching position.

"Why don't you make friends with the horse? It'd make my life a lot easier. I can see we'll have to teach you a bit o' horse sense." Sean chuckled to himself at his wit.

The next few days Blazer was back in full training. Campbell had decided to take him along to Hennessee's for a bit of exercise, as well as to raise the prize money.

The third day Campbell was a little concerned about the dog's health for he had been rigid and unable to move when Sean looked into the barn first thing in the morning.

"It's all right, Mr. Campbell, he's okay. I've just overdone it a bit for the first couple of days; he's just stiff. His muscles have just tightened." A pit bull terrier will go on and on and it is up to the trainer to realize when the dog has had enough to gain full benefit from his exercise.

"I'll give him a day's rest and then a gentle bit of exercise the next day. He'll be as right as rain."

"Okay, Sean, but take it easy; remember, I've got a lot of money going on this one."

"Don't worry, sir, he'll be fighting fit on Friday."

It was a good turnout at Hennessee's. Watches had been posted and each guest was known.

Campbell arrived a few minutes after the first contestants were being washed.

"Is Brady here?" he enquired of Darren Altoll, the German referee.

"I haf not seen him, Mr. Campbell, but 'ee will I'm sure be here."

Campbell took in the scene. The 'pit' was slightly smaller than the one in England and there was no sawdust or wood shavings down. There was a dividing line across the center of the pit.

The dogs 'competing' were two tough looking warriors both with cropped ears and of dubious lineage. One was stockier and cobbier than the other with well muscled hind legs and broad chest. The other, a red colored, gave the impression of being lean although possessing a large head. Campbell knew that appearance to a certain extent could be misleading and the lean dog was probably as strong and a lot more agile. He had left Blazer outside with Sean while he had come in to find Brady. He went out to the yard where Sean was with Blazer.

"Well, well, Mr. Brady."

Brady was chattering to Sean and patting Blazer's head. Brady, a man of about fifty who had been known in the dog fighting circles for thirty years or so—bald with a large black moustache, had the reputation of knowing what he was talking about.

"Nice dog, Campbell, nice dog. I hear he came from Ireland."

"England."

"Of course; did you see him work?"

"I did and I would be prepared to put money on him against Redbrick Willie."

"How much?" Brady came quickly to the point. He was a man of few words and didn't believe in wasting time with pleasantries.

"Two thousand dollars," replied Campbell.

Sean winced. "This is one hell of an expensive dog," he thought. "God alone knows how much Campbell paid for the mutt and now if he loses it'll cost another two thousand dollars. Saints preserve us!"

"Done," Brady said and bent down to fondle Blazer. "He's a nice looking dog, good head, but I think Red's got the edge."

"We'll see," said Campbell.

"We will indeed, Mr. Campbell, good evening sir, I'll see Altoll and we'll arrange the venue. A meet has been called for February, a place to be arranged."

"Very well," Campbell agreed, "until then."

From within the back room of the store snarls and growls could be heard as the two dogs within set to.

Campbell stroked Blazer's back. Blazer was taut and prepared, totally alert; he could hear the scuffle and wanted to get in.

"Who's he matched against, Mr. Campbell?"

"Ruskin's timber."

"I've never yet met a wolf that could take a good bulldog."

"This one has evidently been doing well."

"Perhaps against a few curs."

"It's a heavy dog, weighs about 110 lbs."

"Twice the weight of Blazer."

"I know, but even so I'd put my money on a 'pit' dog."

The previous fight in the pit took about thirty-five minutes, the red dog eventually getting the edge and forcing the heavier animal into the corner of the pit. When it was time for the heavier dog to scratch, it stood in the corner of the pit trembling from shock. The poor animal just remained still except for the slight vibration of its body, the saliva flecked with blood running from his jowls. The owner of the heavy was obviously annoyed; he picked the dog up and strode out of the pit, the crowd booing and jeering.

"I shouldn't give much for the future of that dog," thought Sean, as he trotted Blazer into the pit. At least Campbell wouldn't destroy his dogs if they didn't come up to scratch. He wouldn't breed from them again, although most owners destroyed dogs that showed poor quality in order to ensure that only the best come through.

There was a distinct odor of dogs mixed with human sweat and alcohol as Campbell and Sean went to the corner. The betting had come down heavily in favor of Blazer although no one as yet had seen him. The wolf had to be held and netted, the animal still being very wild. The frightened creature had fought not because he wanted to fight but because he had found himself in the terrifying situation of being in an enclosed space surrounded by shouting human beings and fear had been his motivation. Upon seeing another hostile animal he had taken the only alternative: to defend himself. The wolf had been released first and the referee had stepped out of the pit although he was armed with a heavy club.

After Blazer had been examined, he was dropped into the pit. Immediately his feet had touched ground, Blazer shot across toward the large wolf. The wolf remained still and sidestepped the dog's rush and slashed at Blazer's flanks as he passed. The hard muscled shoulder took the full impact of the wolf's fangs and the wolf's head was jerked sideways as the weight of Blazer went forward. Blazer moved in again. The wolf's fangs slashed again at Blazer's head, the teeth clipping the top off of one of Blazer's ears. Blazer took no notice but bored into the attack. The wolf was obviously an intelligent fighter and had remained alive only because of his tactics. A less experienced dog might

Blazer fighting the wolf

have continued to be out maneuvered and suffered heavy damage and perhaps even losing so much blood that the fight would have been lost.

Although Blazer had never encountered a wolf before, he had fought a good number of dogs and knew if he couldn't get to the throat or shoulder there were alternatives. Blazer charged again; the wolf turned away and slashed as Blazer went through, but this time Blazer, instead of returning to attack the front of the wolf, continued his thrust forward and as he passed, ignored the slashing fangs, turned inward and took the wolf's hind leg crushing as hard as his steel jaws could. The wolf cried out a spiteful yelp. Blazer released the stifle and turned to face the wolf. The wolf jumped away and faced the snarling Blazer who went in low. The wolf slashed once and twice at Blazer's head and shoulders. But it was too late; the steel jaws had clamped solidly onto the wolf's throat and rolled him over.

"It's all over," Campbell shouted.

The crowd was yelling encouragement at Blazer.

"Get him off, Sean."

"Aye, Mr. Campbell."

The trapper who had set the wolf in the pit now was disinterested. The animal had been beaten and it was unlikely that he'd have much stomach for a fight in the future. He turned and left.

Campbell shouted at him, "Net your animal and I'll get mine off him."

"It's up to you. I do not want zis creature."

Campbell cursed the man.

"Give me the net. Sean, you grab Blazer. Careful of his neck though he's got a couple of gashes."

The wolf's head was netted and the referee held it as Campbell and Sean pried Blazer off. Eventually he broke his grip. Sean took him away. Campbell and the referee held the wolf in the net.

"What are you going to do with him?" Campbell asked.

"Shoot him. He's not much good now."

Poor creature, Campbell thought, he didn't want to be here, he had no natural desire to fight. Campbell had always liked wolves despite their sometimes costly eating habits—a much maligned animal, he thought.

The wolf in the net struggled for a few moments and then remained still. The eyes closed and the heart stopped beating.

"Looks like he's saved you the cost of a bullet," Campbell remarked sarcastically.

The spectators filed out, a few of them stopping to look at the dead wolf.

Campbell had felt sorry for the animal and had already decided to obtain it from the trapper and release it. A friend of his was always going back and forth to timber wolf country and could have taken it for him. "Oh well," he thought, "the Road to Hell is paved with good intentions." Pit dogs loved to fight, were bred to fight; wolves and other creatures were not.

That's the last time Blazer takes a wolf," Campbell resolved.

After a meet the spectators don't usually hang around, for obvious reasons, but just as Campbell was going towards his buggy, a voice called out to him from the darkness. It was Brady.

"Care to make it three thousand, Campbell?"

"If you wish," although Campbell was a little taken aback at this display of confidence and also just after Blazer had fought.

"He's not a bad dog, but after having seen him, I think Red will prove the better."

"Well, we're all entitled to our opinion, Mr. Brady," Campbell replied.

"Three thousand it is then; good night." Campbell whipped up his horse; he was anxious to get back to check Blazer. Perhaps Brady knew something I didn't, he thought.

Chapter 3

On his way back to the estate, his mind dwelled upon the whole subject of dog fighting—the way he hated to see an animal in pain and yet thrilled at the thought of two supreme athletic dogs proving their courage, strength and tenacity. It was like a lot of hunters he knew. They would shoot a fowl or an animal and yet if they came across one with a broken limb they would take endless trouble to ensure its recovery. When eventually Campbell arrived at the estate he was greeted by an anxious Sean.

"Mr. Campbell, sir, Blazer's gone. I brought him back here in the buggy, put him in the barn, went over the house to get some water to wash him and when I came back, the barn door was ajar and there was no sign of him."

"Where have you looked?"

"All around, sir, he couldn't have gone far. The bleeding of his shoulder had stopped and his ear had also clotted, so there's no blood trail."

"Well, you wouldn't see it anyway, it's pitch black. There's not a lot we can do—get his dish, put some food in it and leave the barn door ajar. We'll have a look around first and then we'll see what happens."

"I'm sorry, Mr. Campbell, sir. I'm sure I locked the barn door."

"What's done is done, Sean. Prepare his dinner anyway. I shouldn't think he would have gone far. He'll be back."

When Sean had put Blazer into the barn and gone over to the house to get some water, the dog had stiffly crossed the barn and lay down on his sacking bed. He had barely been there a few seconds when he was aware of a shuffling and scratching at the door. The dog had leapt up and gone over to the door to investigate. The scratching on the other side of the door had continued and then the door had swung ajar. There, framed in the lantern light in the barn, which Sean had left, was the silhouette of a dog. Blazer's hackles had instantly gone up and then relaxed as he recognized the scent. It was Bess wagging her tail and lowering her face as she came over to Blazer. She sensed that he had wounds and cautiously sniffed at them. Blazer remained still. The two dogs completed their formalities and then Bess turned toward the open door and ran through. Blazer hesitated for a moment. He was tired and hungry, although not exhausted, but the bitch got the better of him and he raced out after her.

The two dogs ran into the darkness and out into the countryside. It was a new experience for Blazer; he had always been restrained or had a man with him on any venture out of his backyard. Although his wounds were sore and his ear was tender, he ran after Bess, keeping up with her. He stopped once at a stream and lapped some water. Bess waited and then ran on when he had completed his drink. The night was cold and clear and the stars twinkled in the heavens as the two dogs gamboled through the countryside. Bess was familiar with the land and all its accompanying sights and sounds; she ignored cattle and sheep and took not the slightest interest in horses or fowl. For Blazer, it was different. When he came upon a horse face to face in the open without restraint, he stood stock-still and snarled animosity. Bess barked, jumping at him and nipping his tail. Blazer ignored her. He ran at the horse. The animal seemed to get bigger as he approached and just stood his ground. He ran around it looking for a place to attack. The horse with dignity raised its head and pricked its ears forward. Blazer leapt up at the enormous animal, snarling. He tried to sink his teeth into its side as the impact of his body hit the horse. The horse's ears went back and it bucked and kicked. The hoofs missed Blazer by a hair's breadth. He felt the rush of wind over his head as the rock-like feet lashed out. The horse then took off along a clearly delved path visible in the darkness. Blazer followed, with Bess barking her disapproval at him.

The horse cantered into a stretch of land where there were other horses grazing. The animals all looked up as the newcomer thundered into their

Blazer attacks the horse

midst with the dog at his heels. Blazer rushed headlong into the middle of them. He was now confused. There were about a dozen of them to sort out and he didn't know which one to go for, so he chose the one nearest to him. As the dog snapped and snarled at the heels of the horse, the animal would break out into a reluctant canter, circle a few times and then rejoin the group. This way Blazer kept chasing a fresh horse each time.

Bess had already settled down in a corner of the pasture to wait. Eventually Blazer stopped and the horses continued to browse through the autumnal grasses. He was totally exhausted. He stood staring at the horses who were now ignoring him, his tongue lolling from the side of his mouth, and his ribcage pumping away, taking in lungfuls of air. Bess came alongside the stationary dog; she licked his torn ear. Blazer sank down on his stomach, pushing his hind legs out straight behind him. He pulled the weight of his body forward on his front legs dragging his stomach through the cooling grass, stood up, barked at the nearest horse, turned round and trundled after Bess. The dogs travelled high up into wooded country.

Blazer was tired and now beginning to get hungry. Bess was often away from Arnot's place for several days. Arnot had long since given up trying to contain her or use her for work, and it was only because his daughter loved her that he hadn't destroyed her. So he had resigned himself to the fact that she was useless and treated her as a pet of Mary's. The only thing he had done was destroy the two litters of pups that she had given birth to. One thing was for sure—he didn't want any more like her.

The dawn had broken and Blazer experienced the coming of light, shivering in the cool air. There had been no snow but the winter was well on its way, the golden fingers of the sun as they crept through the misty morning contained but a watery warmth. The two dogs sniffed the chill air and watched a flock of duck scud through the sky above them. Bess licked Blazer's flank and tenderly cleansed the clipped ear.

He was feeling tired and turned away towards an overhanging rock that went into a small cave affording some shelter from the cold. Bess watched the white dog shuffle away from her and disappear into the blackness of the cave. There was a mild scuffling sound, a dull thud, and deep sigh as Blazer settled down. He was soon asleep. Bess was feeling hungry and as was her usual way after being out all night or away from home, she would return to the farm for her food and a bowl of fresh milk supplied by little Mary. She looked into the blackness of the cave and barked; nothing stirred; she peered within the gloom. Blazer opened one eye and closed it again. Bess barked once more; again Blazer ignored her. She continued her barking for a few minutes and then turned around on her heels and ran towards the farm.

Her instincts guided her in the direction of the Arnot spread and she raced down the track towards her bowl of fresh milk. As she ran through the dull morning her nose caught the scent of fresh killed meat. She slowed down and tasted the air. It was sheep. She had never eaten sheep but she knew the smell of freshly killed lamb. She stopped in the wooded track and crossed under a low wooden fence into the grazing pastures. Several sheep scattered as she entered the field. She barked at a nearby ram and ran into the center of the flock at the end of the field; she could see the author of the scent she had caught along the forest track. There at the far end of the paddock was a dead lamb, but even more surprisingly, a large member of the cat family was eating a piece of the animal's flesh. It was a lynx—a large one at that. She had never seen one before but her instincts told her that the animal was up to no good and the pungent feline odor made the hairs on the back of her neck bristle.

She raced across the paddock, barking at the cat. The lynx stopped tearing at the flesh and stiffened as the dog neared. The back arched and he gave a low growl. Bess kept on going. As she finally got to the cat she circled 'round growling and snapping. The lynx spat out at her and aimed a savage blow with his forepaw. The rear sharp claws still entangled with wool from the dead lamb missed the dog by inches. The lynx flattened to the ground, its ears went back, the lips curled over the white teeth and the cruel yellow eyes narrowed. Bess darted in and around the crouching animal. The sheep, bewildered by all the noise and commotion, huddled together in the corner of the field, watching. Suddenly, without warning the lynx charged. Bess tried to turn to avoid the spitting fury but the steel claws raked into her flanks and the jaws bit deep into her shoulders. The two animals rolled over and over snarling, scratching, and tearing. It was this scene that Blazer, racing down the hill towards the sound

Blazer races toward the lynx

of the furor, came upon. The sight of the lynx spurred him on even faster. His wounds from the fight with the wolf were still red and exposed and he was tired and hungry but all these were forgotten as he launched himself into the fray.

The lynx glimpsed sight of Blazer and released his hold on Bess. Blazer caught the lynx off balance as it turned to face him. The full weight of the bull terrier's solid fighting muscle thudded into the cat; the steel jaws found the lynx's throat and closed unmercifully. The lynx rolled over in the wet grass, the fur looking blacker as it got wetter; the front paws of the lynx grasped Blazer and the powerful hind legs ripped into his body. The bull terrier held firm. The lynx's scathing hind legs again pumped furiously leaving red claw marks on the belly and underside of Blazer. The bull terrier held firm. Eventually the tearing became less furious and the cat's steel taut body slackened and became limp, the breathing stopped and the beautiful yellow eyes closed in death.

Chapter 4

Ben Rearden plodded across the field, his rifle crooked in his arm and his dog Bofors running ahead. Bofors barked and yelped excitedly as he came upon the prostrate animals.

"Well I'll be, looks like a—come out of it, Bofors." The man surveyed the scene before him. Lying next to the half eaten sheep was Bess lifeless in the grass, her torn body stretched out as asleep. Next to her lay the lynx and firmly affixed to his throat was the bull terrier scarred and ripped, his body one red mass of torn flesh.

"Seems, Bofors, there's been some kinda' brawl here, looks like they've all had it. Hey, wait a minute." Ben thought he saw Blazer's eye flicker. Bofors was growling and snarling at the dead lynx.

"You're a bit late, boy. Yeah, this is one we've been after—the one that escaped about a fortnight ago from the Green's spread. That bloke Green ought to have knowed better, danged idiot." Ben spat contemptuously into the grass.

"Let's have a look at you, boy." Rearden maneuvered himself to Blazer's head; he laid his rifle down and lifted the dog's head still locked solidly onto the lynx's throat. "Come on, boy, if yer've still got life in yer; let go—there's a good un."

The jaws still held solid.

"Danged blast it, I'm trying not to hurt yer, you've got to let go. Bofors, come nearer to him."

Perhaps it was instinct or perhaps Blazer knew the animal was dead, but he slackened his grip and Rearden managed to pry the jaws apart and release the cat. Bofors sniffed Blazer's head. Blazer, although totally still and unable to move, just managed a snarl from a turned up lip, warning Bofors.

"That's enough of that, yer blame cur. Yer in no condition to be cocky." Rearden lay Blazer's head in the grass and went over to Bess.

"Well, Bofors, she's a gonna, I'm afraid. Come on, let's get this one back to the farm, although I don't suppose he'll last the night." Rearden covered Blazer with a blanket that he'd bought for extra warmth and carefully picked the dog up, keeping him as rigid as possible.

"Jeez, you're a weight, I'll never manage you for three miles. I'll have to go and get the buggy. You stay here, Bofors, and look after him. I'll be back within the hour."

Rearden commanded Bofors to stay and started off down the hill. About two hours passed and Rearden reappeared. Bofors had stayed close to the bull terrier watching him as he lay in the grass breathing faintly underneath the blanket, the watery sun hardly drying the blood on the once white coat. Bofors leapt up as he heard the sound of horses' hooves and the rattle of the cart wheels grinding their way toward them. He went across to Rearden and ran around him excitedly.

"Okay. Bofors, okay. I see he's still here. I guess I'll take that sheepdog back as well, try and find out who's she was." Rearden carefully loaded the bull terrier onto the buck board along with the sheepdog, climbed aboard and started back towards his farm.

"Come on, Bofors let's git." He clipped the horse's rump with the reins and the animal strained in the shafts. The cart rumbled off down the track.

Rearden mused as to what he was going to do with this dog if it survived. Jessie, his wife, was good with animals and she'd cared for several of the livestock that had been sick in the past. They lived in a small cabin with about 44 acres approximately fourteen miles from Campbell's spread. Rearden knew of Campbell, but hadn't seen him for several months and did not know that Blazer belonged to him. Rearden scratched up a living by farming; he had a few cows and several pigs. He was self-sufficient and traded what surplus he had on infrequent visits to Boston and with local farmers.

After about an hour the wagon trundled along a track beside a stream and Rearden could see the smoke winding up from his cabin. His wife was outside hanging out some clothes, several chickens scratched about in the yard in front of the house and a goat eyed them as they approached. Rearden stopped the wagon and climbed down. Jessie Rearden came over to him.

"Where's the dog?"

"In the back."

Jessie peered into the buckboard.

"Hm, looks kinda chewed up."

"Yeh, I don't reckon he'll make it."

"Maybe," Jessie replied. "Here, give me a hand and let's get him over to the barn."

"Might be a shade cold."

"Reckon yer may be right; guess he'd better stay inside for a couple of nights until we know which way he's gonna go. Who's the other dog?"

"I dunno, I reckon it could be Arnot's dog. I've seen her once before but danged if I can remember where."

They lifted Blazer from the buckboard and took him inside. Jessie warmed some water and applied a soft cloth gently to his wounds.

"Looks like some o' these wounds were done afore; some are older."

"He kinda looks like a ploughed field," Rearden mused as he puffed his pipe and watched his wife cleanse the dried blood from Blazer's body.

"Well, I got work to do Jess, see yer later." Rearden left the cabin, whistled to Bofors, and set about his daily chores.

That night Jessie sat in the rocking chair in front of the fire knitting. Blazer was stretched out on a rug near the hearth. Rearden sat opposite drawing on his pipe, Bofors asleep at his feet.

"I'll take off over to Arnot's place sometime in the next couple of days and see if it was his dog. I don't know about the whit'un, he's I would think a pit

Jessie Rearden tending to the lynx-wounded Blazer

dog. Those mean devils setting dogs to fight against one another, he'll not fight while he's around me."

"He's got a fight on his hands right this minute."

"Aye, yer right Jessie."

Blazer remained still in front of the glowing embers, his breathing just visible, his ribs rising and falling slowly.

Chapter 5

It was about a week before Blazer showed any real signs of recovery. He had remained virtually motionless for about two days, Jessie sweeping and cleaning around him. It was on the evening of the third day that he painfully raised himself and shuffled toward the door. Jessie understood his desire and opened the door for him; the dog hobbled down the steps of the cabin, stood motionless gazing into the air with a blank vacant expression and, without a sound, relieved himself. After having completed this function, he stiff-leggedly turned himself around, negotiated the steps with a certain amount of difficulty, wagged his tail half-heartedly in acknowledgment of Jessie's presence, and staggered back to the fireplace; with a thump, his body hit the rug and there he stayed. Jessie put some warm milk down for him which he lapped with as

Blazer recuperating in front of the Reardens' fireplace

much enthusiasm as he could muster. She also dropped some lean raw meat with a little bread which she put down next to the dog, if and when he needed it. After the fourth day Blazer began to benefit from the meat; the wounds, still visibly painful and obviously causing him discomfort, were lean and therefore not septic. The fact that he had eaten was an indication that he was on the slow but sure road to recovery.

Rearden had not as yet got around to visiting Arnot's spread, although the mystery had been solved by the visit of Sean who had ridden in to ask if he had seen Blazer. Sean had spoken of the dog to Rearden after he had declined to come in and take some refreshment.

"Mr. Campbell's top dog is missing and there's a big reward to be had if yer can give any information."

Rearden was not averse to money and was about to mention the dog to Sean before Sean had mentioned it to him but held his counsel. Instead he asked,

"What kind of dog was this top dog?"

"A dog he brought over from England. A bulldog. He was right fond of it an' all." Sean used the term bulldog because he was sure Rearden would not know anything about the finer points of fighting dogs. He also didn't mention the fact that Campbell brought the dog specifically for this purpose. Rearden on the other hand knew exactly what he meant and also knew that if he gave the dog to Sean the animal would be back in the dog pit in no time.

"Why should he think I've seen it?"

"Well he don't; he's just asking all the neighboring spreads to keep a lookout and if anyone sees the dog and it's worrying any sheep or anything, not to shoot it but to catch it alive and Mr. Campbell will make good any damage."

"He must think a lot of this critter."

"He does that," Sean replied. "Well, I'll be going then."

Rearden patted Sean's horse and hoped that Jessie wouldn't come out and press Sean to come inside and have some refreshment.

"Nice seeing yer."

"Aye, regards to Mrs. Rearden."

Sean dug his heels into the horse's flanks and the creature shot forward. The bulk of the animal thundered off into the distance.

Jessie came out just as Sean was riding away.

"Didn't he want to come in? I've got some fresh bread and some pie with ale ready."

"No he's looking for Campbell's dog, that same critter that's stretched out in front of our fire. It's as I thought, he's been using him in the pit."

"Shame on Campbell! What did you tell him?"

"Nothing. I didn't say I hadn't seen him and I didn't say I had."

And so it was that Blazer recovered with the warmth of Rearden's fireside and the food given by Jessie. In his fighting trim Blazer was sometimes eating over three pounds of meat a day and still remaining lean. Now he was eating about a pound and a half and putting on weight. His relationship with Bofors was one of friendship. Bofors was not an aggressive dog and Blazer had known of his presence next to him while he was recovering. At first, when Bofors had approached the sleeping dog, Blazer had growled warningly but after several days Bofors would lie almost next to the scarred dog without even a growl and so gradually, as Blazer recovered, he accepted the presence of the sheepdog without question as being the order of things.

Unfortunately he was not the same with the livestock and killed two fowl before Rearden realized his disposition. Rearden constructed a kennel and wired off a run so that Blazer could be contained and left during the day. In the evening he was allowed to run free with Bofors and the two dogs would race around the small holding, thundering through puddles, racing around the paddock. Blazer, although hardly friendly with horses now, just gave them a bark as he raced.

〰〰〰〰〰

Then the winter came and went. Blazer's scars still remained like pink strips on the underside of his belly, his ear neatly clipped and his head had a distinct chewed look about it. He no longer slept in the house, although he was warm and dry in the shelter Rearden had constructed.

Spring was in the air and Rearden was kept busy with his lambs and keeping the small holding going.

It was now May. The brownish gray wintery look of the countryside had given way to the warm green freshness of early summer, of blossoms on the trees, of the sound of young fledglings and the drone of bees. It was a time of year that meant work for Rearden and Bofors but the atmosphere of the world, the freshness, made it a joy to be outside.

Simms and Grey come to see Mr. Rearden at his farm

It was about mid-morning on one of these sweet smelling days that Simms and Grey, two no-goods who dealt in furs, guns, farm equipment or anything they could lay their hands on, turned up. It was their custom to do the rounds of the farms and homesteads to see if any of the settlers needed anything. Rearden had bought a carpet from one of them once and ever since they had paid their annual visit. He was in the fields when they came along the stream and entered his property. Blazer was in his enclosure and stood up and barked through the mesh. Simms caught sight of the dog and nudged Grey.

"Eh, looks like a pig, don't it?"

"Eh, wait a minute, ain't that the dog that that Irishman was on about, it's white, pig-like eyes."

"Yeah, could be. Wasn't there a reward?"

"Yeah. Perhaps it ain't the same one."

Simms walked over to Blazer who had by now stopped barking and was wagging his tail as Simms approached.

"Fine guard dog, ain't he," Simms laughed sarcastically.

At that moment as Simms was poking his fingers through the mesh of Blazer's enclosure Jessie Rearden, hearing Blazer bark, came out of the cabin.

"What can I do for yers, gentlemen?"

Simms swung round, slightly caught off balance, as if his thoughts had been laid bare.

"Oh greetings, Mrs. Rearden, is Rearden about? We've come to see if he needs anything, a good rifle, another rug, a few snares?"

"I don't think so, he's been a-meaning to go into town in the next couple of days for a few supplies."

"Oh, thank yer kindly mam,—er may I just ask—
that's an odd looking cur he's got there."

Mrs. Rearden saw the look between the two unshaven men; she could almost smell their dirty
clothes from where she stood. She couldn't tell
them it was Blazer whom Campbell was looking for.
News travels fast and she knew that Campbell
would come and get him virtually within hours of
hearing of the dog's whereabouts. She blamed Rearden for turning Blazer outside where he could be
seen. Although they rarely had visitors, it was not
unusual for people to drop in on their way to and
from neighboring homesteads; after all a lot of
them were related through marriage and were
proud of their Pilgrim Fathers' heritage.

It was against her nature to lie; she thought for a
few seconds trying to explain how Blazer got there.

" 'Cos he sure looks like a cur that a certain Mr.
Campbell from the big spread east of here lost
some months ago."

"Well now fancy—Rearden found him a few
months back, perhaps that would be him."

"Would yer like us to take him off yer hands and
give him back to Campbell?"

"No, no I'll tell Rearden when he gets back. You
can have a coffee and a piece of pie afore yer go."

"Thank yer kindly, mam, sounds generous of
you."

The two men sat on the steps eating the freshly
baked apple pie and drinking their coffee. Blazer
could smell the pastry and gave a bark that more
resembled a yap. Grey tossed a piece of the pastry
into Blazer's pen. Blazer wolfed it down.

"It don't even touch the sides," Grey sniggered.

"Yeah. Now then what do you think we should do about this cur?"

"How do you mean, Simms?"

"I think we should return this dog from where it came—a kinda civil duty yer might say."

"Seems a shame to throw away such good pie," Simms smirked. "Good pie."

"Are yer going?" Simms nudged Grey. "Joke, get it? Yer said good pie, good bye."

"Yea, yea, very funny. Now listen, I don't think we'd have any problems taking the dog; he seems a might too friendly for his own good."

"Yeah."

Simms and Grey thanked Jessie Rearden for her hospitality and left. Jessie trusted neither of them and when Rearden and Bofors returned that evening she set his supper down and told him of the day's events.

"Hmmm," Rearden exclaimed, "seems like we'll have to do something now. Campbell is bound to find out. He was offering a reward and types like Simms and Grey won't let a chance like that slip by them."

Blazer had eaten and was at the moment racing through the paddock gate in pursuit of Bofors. Bofors had been on his feet all day and had covered several miles during the course of his work; nonetheless he was still game and enjoyed his romp with Blazer.

Simms and Grey had stayed close to the cabin, but well out of sight; they had watched Rearden trudge across from the pig pen on his way from the fields, release Blazer from his enclosure and wearily enter the cabin. Blazer had acknowledged his presence with one quick tail wag and darted out after the sheepdog—the two dogs raced off in the direction of where Simms and Grey were watching. Bofors had come upon them first.

"Well, lookee here. The Lord is smiling on us today."

"Eh, it couldn't have been better." The two villains went into action.

"Comere boy, there's a good fella."

"Comere you 'orrible pig eye git."

"Simms, have some respect, ee might be gittin' 'iself upset."

Blazer went up to Simms wagging his tail.

"There's a good boy."

Blazer had never had any reason to dislike men; he had always been fed by them and because of them he got to do what he liked best. He had never formed a close bond with any of his owners perhaps because they were never over-demonstrative or perhaps it was because he was the dog he was. He liked Rearden, wagged his tail and licked his face, but would never pine if he never saw either him or Jessie again. Which was perhaps just as well because at that particular time in his life this was what was about to happen. Bofors, on the other hand, was not as pleasantly disposed to strangers as was Blazer, being a herding and also guard dog. He approached the two villains with a different attitude. He stopped short of them and began barking and snarling.

"Get out of it, go on, git," Simms snarled.

"Here, keep hold of this one." Simms gave Blazer, who was now roped by the neck, to Grey.

Blazer approaches Simms and Grey

Bofors barked louder and darted at Simms' feet. Simms kicked out viciously, his boot caught Bofors firmly in the ribs and lifted him off the ground; the dog landed several feet away. The blow had knocked the wind out of him and he let out an involuntary squeal of pain. Simms ran over to him and quickly drew his knife. Bofors saw him coming and although in pain ran off back to the cabin.

"Blast, dang blast it." Simms cursed and hurled his knife at Bofors; the blade bounced harmlessly against a tree and thudded to the ground making a puff of dust as the handle made contact with the earth.

"Come on, Simms, let's git," Grey snapped. "We've got the cur."

"Yeah, but I wanted to finish that mongrel off—it just means we'll have to travel faster."

"Okay, but let's go."

The two men collected their items of trading value and slung them in a small cart they took with them. Blazer trotted behind them as they made their way back in the direction of Campbell's.

" 'E'll give us good money."

"Yeah, where did we find him?"

"Well we can tell the truth, he came up to us just outside of Rearden's place."

"Yeah he did."

"That's what I said," Simms pursed his lips and spat a stream of saliva as he did occasionally to emphasize a point.

"How long do yer reckon it'll take us to git back?"

"I want to call in on Treeves afore we go to Campbell ."

"Why Simms, wouldn't it be best to get the reward first?"

"Aye, but Treeves owes me money and I know I'm going to get that for sure."

The two men trundled on in the dusk, the cartwheels creaking in the still summer evening, Blazer tied to the cart walking after them.

It was about four hours later that the two men came in sight of a small cabin, a light shining from within.

"Ah well, at least he's in," Simms remarked. "Maybe he's got some grub. I'm getting kinda hungry, kept thinking how we ain't likely to get Mrs. Rearden's apple pie for some time to come."

The summer night was warm and Simms punctuated his words with a slap of his hand against an exposed part of his anatomy.

"Danged 'squitoes dang blast, if ever I knowed why they was made, seems like just to annoy you."

Grey chuckled. "They don't bother me none."

"Yeah, well, you're too danged tough skinned." Simms raised his unshaven face and yelled out as they approached the cabin.

"Hey, Treeves you son of a bitch, it's us—put on some coffee and grub."

The door of the cabin creaked open and in the light stood a man of about fifty, unshaven and dishevelled, a ginger beard sprouting unevenly from his chin; he wore a thick shirt and a buckskin jacket. In his hand he held a double barrelled shotgun. "Who's there?" he called.

"It's me—Simms."

"And me, Grey."

Treeves lowered the shotgun.

"Well, well, the last persons I ever expected to see, I don't think. What kept you?"

"Now come on, Treeves, don't be like that."

The two men parked their hand wagon and trundled up the steps to the cabin.

"Better come inside then."

"Mighty nice of you. Any chow?"

"I've got a few beans and some coffee."

"No liquor?" Simms cast a glance at the table where a bottle stood.

"Yer welcome to it."

Grey stretched out his arms and put the stem of the bottle up to his mouth; he took a long swig, retained the liquid in his mouth, his face twisted with disbelief and sprayed the contents of his mouth over Simms.

"What the—Grey, you son of a bitch."

"Water," Grey exclaimed "filthy water."

"I never said it was anything else," Treeves remarked.

Simms wiped his hand over his shirt.

"You filthy low down."

"I'm sorry, Simms, I just got taken by surprise."

"Yeah, okay. Let's git some grub." Simms muttered some obscenity.

Treeves went to a cupboard and produced an ancient tin of beans and a couple of metal plates. The cabin was filthy; a table and two chairs took up the largest part of the space and several tins and empty bottles littered the floor. The light from a lamp flickered over the room.

"What about the cur?"

"Better take a look, Grey."

In Treeves's cabin

"What cur?" Treeves asked, "I thought I seen a dog aback that junk wagon of yours."

"Yeah, well he's worth money."

"How come?"

"He belongs to a man called Campbell who kinda likes him a lot."

"Campbell, yeah, I know the Campbell spread and I know the dog. I've seen him."

Treeves got up from the cabin and went outside. Grey was outside patting Blazer's head while Blazer was wagging his tail.

"That's him all right," Treeves remarked, "I saw him some months ago against a wolf."

"That's right, then Campbell lost him, he was going up against Brady's Red, then he vanished."

"I get it now, you're going for the reward. Where did yer find him?"

"He just came up to us this evening and we recognized him from the description."

"You mean out o' the blue he just walked up to you?"

"Well, yeah, Rearden had been lookin' after him for us until we arrived."

"Hmmm, anyway what are you going to do with him, just give him back?"

"Yeah, why not?"

"I was just thinking. A man called Fenton about 100 miles north of here has been breedin' dogs that he rates high, high enough to put a big price on against another."

"I ain't ever seen these curs but I hear he's mixed a few big breeds into one mighty mean beast."

"Like what?" Simms enquired, knowing nothing about dog breeds or dog fighting.

"Them lean hounds, mastiff, bulldog, and pit dog and they're big."

"How'd he go against one?" Simm nodded toward Blazer.

"Fenton reckons one of his dogs break him in half in no time flat."

"Yeah maybe he's right."

"Maybe he's wrong, he's got good money to back him."

"But Treeves, we ain't got no money to back this one, talkin' of which you owes me."

"I thought you'd never get around to it."

"Listen, do yer fancy making some money out of this cur against Fenton's?"

"What about Campbell?" Grey interrupted.

"It's easy money and half the travel. I can't stomach a 100 mile trek; by the time we got there the dog'd be too danged blasted tired out to fight a racoon let alone one of Fenton's critters."

"Grey's got a point, Treeves."

"If we return the dog to Campbell, he'll give us a couple of hundred dollars and we don't have no aggravation. If we go up to Fenton's we risk losing the dog and the money."

"Listen, if you go up to Fenton's you can always bring the dog back again and return him to Campbell when it's over regardless of whether he wins or loses. That way you're guaranteed the money. Campbell never stated the condition of the dog." Treeves argued.

"Yeah, there's only one small point, what's going to stake us against Fenton's dog?"

"Hmm, well I got a little bit stashed."

"Oh, yeah, and it's going to be smaller after you've given us our fifty dollars."

"Okay, okay you'll get your fifty dollars but I was thinking more in the way of a trader I know who don't like Fenton and would be willin' to stake us to bring him into line."

"That's all very well but say this mutt don't win. It means we've spent a lot of time, effort and dough for nothing, when we could easily just hand him over to Campbell and be sure of gittin' the reward." Grey emphasized his point by smacking his gnarled fist into the palm of his hand.

"You're talking about a few paltry hundreds against thousands, that's why. If the mutt wins we could perhaps be open to offers."

"Yeah, I never thought of that," Grey replied, "Yeah, okay let's take a gamble, but what about food and travel and surely he'll be tired out the time he gits there."

"Not if we take it slow," Treeves remarked. "We ain't in no hurry and we can feed him on a few supplies and what we shoot; anyhow's dogs need walkin'; it does 'em good."

"Not a 100 mile one though," Grey interrupted.

"Well let's get bedded down and finish them beans, the mutt can sleep in the cabin with us, and what about his grub, has he had any?"

"Reckon Rearden would have fed him."

"Yeah, we'll git him some fresh rabbit tomorrow. Got to keep his strength up, after all he's a mighty valuable critter."

The three men and the dog went inside the cabin and the door banged shut.

Starting off on the trip

The journey north started a little later than planned. Treeves went out rabbit shooting first thing and failed to shoot any rabbits so he ended up in desperation shooting a buzzard which he plucked and drew and cut up and gave to Blazer. The dog sniffed the unpleasant looking mass of chopped meat and left it untouched.

"You ungrateful son of a — you lousy . . . ."

"Okay speak nice to him," Simms yelled. "Would you eat a goddam buzzard?"

"Listen, I seen dogs eat things that it makes me sick even to mention. He turns up his nose at fresh meat—he ain't gonna survive the next few days."

The three men pressed northward, to their destination. On their journey they encountered a swarthy Irishman on his way to New York who, upon seeing the dog, started talking about the dog fights in New York and in Ireland. Treeves and Simms listened attentively.

"Of course, if yer was going to fight him he'd have to lose weight and get fit, but I can sees yer ain't. He looks as though he's seen a few scraps to be sure."

"How do you mean lose weight, should we starve him?"

"Lord, no. Yer do that an' he'll be weak. No, he'd have to be trained like."

"Trained? I thought it was natural for 'em to have a go."

"Sure it's natural all right, but yer want to give yer dog the best chance to win."

"Where are yer going?"

"Well," Simms interrupted, "we're just heading north."

"Well good luck, don't forget plenty of food and plenty of exercise."

The Irishman picked up his bed roll, took a swig from a flask he was carrying and strode off.

The trio had covered about forty miles of their journey and were debating what to do for the best.

"Listen, I still say we should have got rid of this mutt to Campbell," Grey argued.

"Quit moaning, we decided to go on and go on we will."

"Well, one thing is for sure; he's going to git plenty of exercise all this walking—yeah maybe we should chuck a couple of sticks for him to run after."

The food problem had been solved. Treeves and Grey had come across an unbranded cow which Blazer had rushed at and clamped onto one of its ears.

"He sure don't like cows," Grey remarked.

"Seems like he does," Treeves grinned, "Take a look. It ain't got no mark on it."

"Yer right, must be wild. Yeah, well, let's tame it."

Grey raised his rifle and shot the cow which sank to its knees with Blazer still clamped onto its ear. Blazer's eyes moved in the direction of the sound of the shot but his grip remained firm. The weight of the dog pulled the cow's bulk over to his side as it crumpled up.

"Hey, git the dog from under that steak, otherwise he'll git rolled on."

Grey rushed up to the cow and fired another shot point blank at its head. The animal's head jerked under the impact of the bullet. Blazer's eyes narrowed and his chewed ear stiffened, but his jaws remained clamped shut on the unfortunate creature's ear.

Grey and Treeves pushed the cow away from Blazer's body and it collapsed motionless.

"Well, the meat shortage is over." Simms grinned as he took out his knife.

"Yeah, how long is that blamed critter gonna hang on to its ear?"

Blazer perhaps realizing that the animal was dead released his grip and rushed excitedly around the large corpse, sniffing, wagging his tail, and barking. The scent of the cow's blood had seemed to stimulate the dog. He took hold of the outstretched tail and shook it vigorously growling and snarling.

The men laughed at the dog.

"Sure does have a sense o' humor, don't he?"

"The thing that worries me is that there seems to be more to this dog scrapping than meets the eye. The Irishman was talking about training and rules and the Lord knows what. We don't know one end of the dog from the other, let alone one kind of mutt."

"That Irishman said something about a bull and terrier or mastiff."

"An' him talking about that massive or whatever it was that killed all them rats, 78 in thirteen minutes in Illinois. Kinda makes yer think."

"Listen," Treeves said, "this trader knows, he knows all about this game, he'll put us right."

"I guess the best thing we can do is to git this critter there in one piece; anyhow let's git this cow butchered and give him some grub. I could do with a steak meself."

"Reckon that ain't a bad idea," Grey agreed.

The cow was duly skinned and cut up, Blazer seizing various pieces of discarded offal and running 'round and 'round with the entrails in his mouth. Simms caught hold of the cow's tail as Blazer ran past him.

"Come here, you son of a bitch. I guess that ain't no insult to him," Simms remarked.

"It ain't to you neither," Grey sniggered.

Blazer came to an abrupt halt and tugged away at the tail with Simms pulling on the other end.

"Kinda playful, ain't he?"

"Yeah, tug harder, he's got to have lots of exercise."

Simms and the dog continued the tug of war with the cow's natural fly swatter until finally Simms picked up the dog and swung him 'round and 'round on the end of the tail.

"Hey Grey, git this. He likes a spin."

Treeves and Grey finally finished the cutting and now Treeves set to making a fire.

"Guess we'll have a bite and then continue."

"Why don't we keep going until dusk and then eat?" Simms said, as he continued to play with Blazer.

"Maybe he's right, Treeves; seems perhaps it's the best to make use of the light and the sooner we meet this trader friend of yours the more we know what's happening."

The three men agreed and set off, the trailer loaded up with fresh meat, although with the abundance of flies and the warmth of the day it wouldn't stay fresh for long. The journey took them just under ten days; nothing eventful happened other than Blazer fell in a creek in pursuit of a couple of ducks and Simms complained that he was nothing but a god blamed jackass. And having to drag a hand cart full of junk and now a dang blasted dead cow which became high after the third day. Blazer had his last meal and a huge bone which he gnarled away on through the night of the fourth day within earshot of Simms who was trying to get some sleep.

The food problem was overcome by Treeves who bought three chickens which he kept alive in a pen perched on the hand wagon and one by one were dispatched as the need arose.

Blazer had taken a liking to Treeves's ginger beard and one evening, when the three men lay in their beds, had smelled food from the particles lodged in the tangled red mass. Treeves had been asleep and had wakened to the odor of dog's breath and a great wet nose buried deep in his chin. His screams awakened Simms and Grey who had seen the humorous side of it.

"Thought ye'd struck lucky," Simms chuckled.

"I bet he was dreamin' about that gal in Boston and the cur's mouth nearly got kissed."

"Dang blast animal, I told yer he should be tied up. Say he takes it in his head to run off—we'll have come this far for nothing and for no reason."

"I wouldn't run away from fresh beef, fresh chicken and plenty of exercise, would you? Besides, it's that beard that really makes him stay, an' he's had the chance enough already. Nevertheless, I reckon we should tie him up to a tree or something."

"Okay, okay," the three men agreed.

Chapter 6

When Bofors had come in that evening Rearden had guessed that something was wrong but hadn't realized because Blazer usually slept out until just before dusk and then returned with Bofors. Bofors had come in and curled up under the table.

"Did yer make sure them chickens were penned up?"

"You know I always do," Jessie Rearden replied.

Rearden had finished his dinner and sat back from the table.

"That was fine Jessie, thank you. I guess I'll have to take that dog to Campbell."

"You can't do that, the dog'll be back fighting in no time."

"Yeah, guess you're right. Well, maybe the best thing is to wait for Campbell or his man to come here and then face it when the time comes."

"Open the door, Jessie, while you're up; it's a mite warm. Hey, Bofors, what's the matter?"

The dog looked up from under the table, wagged his tail once and then rested his head on Rearden's foot.

"Why ain't you with Blazer?"

Rearden stood up and walked over to the open door. The chirping of a cricket came across the still air, a group of mosquitoes danced under the porch and Rearden lazily waved his hand through the insects. Although Sean told Rearden the dog's name when he first came in search of Blazer, Rearden usually called him Boy.

"Hey Boy—here, come here Boy." Rearden gave a shrill whistle.

Bofors leapt up from under the table and stood at Rearden's side.

"Where's Boy, Bofors, find him."

Bofors yelped excitedly and wagged his tail.

"Find him."

Bofors rocketed off across the yard past Blazer's pen and down towards the stream where the two men had been. Rearden strolled from the porch and followed the dog. He took some tobacco from his pouch and filled his pipe.

"Coffee's ready," Jessie called from the cabin.

"Right. Won't be a minute."

The still summer evening and the warmth and peace of it filled Rearden with a sense of well being. He and his wife had no children and his only regret in life was that there would be no heir to carry on with his farm and name.

" 'Tis a pity my son cannot share this with me," he mused.

"Coffee's gittin' cold," Jessie called.

"Comin', put it on the hob, I'm gonna take a stroll by the stream.

Here Boy—here Boy."

Bofors was racing around, his nose close to the ground occasionally looking back to see if Rearden was coming, barking excitedly.

"What's up, Bofors?" Rearden looked down at where Bofors was barking. In the grass were two distinct cart tracks and a patch of flattened grass. Rearden was no Indian Scout but by his reckoning he assumed that someone had been lying in the grass and judging by the flatness, for several hours.

"Now I know them two buzzards came a visitin', but why would they rest up here?"

Rearden nodded, "Of course, waitin' to take the dog—and it looks like they got what they was waitin' for."

"Come on, Bofors, let's get back to the cabin."

When Rearden arrived back at the cabin he explained to Jessie what he had discovered.

"What are ye going to do?"

"Guess I'll go and see Campbell, see if he will part with the dog. I got kind fond of him, although he weren't much of a guard dog and no dang blasted good with stock. I'd like to clear myself with Campbell anyways."

Rearden puffed on his pipe.

"Ain't no use taking after them buzzards, but when I do catch up with 'em they'll know all about it."

"Here's yer coffee."

When Blazer had originally gone with the two men, Simms kept the rope on him and a firm grip on the other end, but Blazer trotted along quite amiably showing no signs of distress. After they left the cabin with Treeves, Blazer spent the first two nights tied to a tree but on the third morning when Simms awoke, the tree where Blazer had been no longer had a dog tied to it.

Simms let out a shout of dismay which woke Treeves and Grey and also the other occupant of Treeves' bunk—a chewed-eared white dog—all four of them stared momentarily at the tree, gazing at the empty space.

"Well, I'll be," said Treeves patting the dog's head. "Guess he likes our company, eh?"

"Yeah, suits me—I don't have to drag him around no more—he can run free an' git some exercise."

After that Blazer trotted along as any dog would—occasionally up front and occasionally staying behind to savor something interesting to him.

Often he would race after a rabbit and return several minutes later panting but with a smile peculiar to bull terriers.

"Bet yer ten dollars he don't git one rabbit between here and this friend o' yours."

"I bet he don't neither," Simms grinned, "I hope he can fight better than he can run."

"Well if he can't run he needs to be able to fight, don't you reckon," Grey chuckled.

It was dusk when the four arrived at a large cabin with a fenced off area at the back, several pots and

93

saucepans hung from the roof along with other articles; the door was closed. Treeves banged on the door. Blazer had just cocked his leg against one of the fence posts when a large black mongrel came racing around the corner snarling and barking at the three men.

"Hold on, yer mangy cur."

The dog stood still, lowered his head and snarled, his lips curled viciously back displaying a superb set of white teeth.

"Don't look too friendly, does he?" Simms remarked.

"Keep still. He won't do nothing."

The first time the black dog saw Blazer was also nearly his last. Blazer had stopped in his tracks and seen the dog facing the three men obviously hostile. Blazer had no idea of protecting the men, but there was an adversary, openly aggressive, looking for trouble. Who knows what goes on in a dog's mind? It certainly doesn't function like that of a man's, but whatever the explanation it was sufficient to stimulate Blazer into action. The white dog rocketed across the space between them, the full weight of his body catching the black dog side on. The wind was audibly knocked out of the mongrel and possibly the fight too. Blazer caught hold of the dog as he rolled over and lifted him back onto his feet and then off them again, slamming the animal to the ground.

Blazer had a powerful shoulder grip and had begun to work his way in and finish the job; the mongrel was squealing with pain.

"Hey, Grey, he danged blamed rescued us."

Blazer takes on McArthur's dog

"Yeah, yeah, don't be fooled anyway, best get him off afore he kills it."

"Let him kill it."

"That's McArthur's dog. I don't think he'll be too pleased if you stand there an' watch."

The door of the cabin opened and out stepped a small stocky man.

"What the hell's going on? Treeves, what are you doing here and what the hell's them dogs doing? Come on, help me break 'em up."

Simms had in the meantime gone over to the two dogs and taken hold of Blazer.

"Come on now, let go, come on."

McArthur stepped down and went over to the dogs, brushing Grey and Treeves aside.

"That ain't no good—take a hold of the black's neck and keep his head away from my hands—when I get this one off, let him go. He won't have no more stomach for fighting."

McArthur lifted Blazer's back legs off the ground and placed them between his knees; then he placed his hand on Blazer's windpipe and squeezed hard. Blazer eventually released his grip and gasped for air. Simms let go of the squealing mongrel who raced off. McArthur still had a grip on Blazer.

"Whose critter's this?"

"Ours," Treeves exclaimed proudly.

"Well, why don't yer keep him off my dog? Put a rope on him while he's here."

Simms produced a rope from the cart and roped Blazer. McArthur released the dog. Blazer was still a little short of air and although he was still looking for the mongrel, he was panting for oxygen.

Treeves said "Come close," to McArthur.

"Let's go inside and have a talk. We've been travelling for a few days and we could do with a drink and something to eat."

"Aye yes, come inside."

McArthur, although a small man, was very powerful and had an abrupt manner, and although it wasn't his intention to appear rude, he usually was. He was a trader by profession and sold everything from tea to tallow. He was also a recognized official at local dog fights and had been interested in the 'sport' for several years. He had in the past bred dogs and fought them although now he assumed the role of referee and judge.

"We came across this dog and seeing as we don't know nothing we came to you," Treeves swigged a glass of whiskey and began to roll a cigarette.

"Yeah, you see," Treeves began.

"You know a lot about curs," Simms eagerly interrupted.

McArthur looked at Simms, his eyes narrowed. It was clear by his expression what he thought of him.

"What's your intention?"

"Well, we was thinking that maybe we could put him against Fenton's cur."

McArthur swung round.

"What! Have you seen Fenton's cur?"

"Well, no."

"Well then, you'd know what I mean when I say I don't think that white 'un would have much chance."

"Why?"

"Well he ain't fighting his own weight for one thing, he's giving away seventy pounds and that's a lot of meat. He'd need to be something special."

"Well, he chewed up that black dog o' yours okay," Simms said.

"Yeah." McArthur dismissed the remark with the contempt he considered it deserved.

"Also you just dragged him 100 miles. That in itself ain't a bad thing but he needs a lot of feed—up to three pounds o' meat a day—as well as tuning up."

"Tuning up?" Simms asked.

"Made ready, so to speak, for the pit then."

"So you don't reckon this mutt of ours could take one of Fenton's dogs?"

McArthur shook his head "I wouldn't like to put money on it, not the one Fenton's using at the moment. It's a big red cur cross all sorts with a lot of pit dog in him."

McArthur crossed to the window and looked out from the back of the cabin where Blazer lay. The light from the window enabled him to see Blazer reasonably well.

"I ain't seen his kind before, although I heard of 'em. Some one in Boston was bringing them over from England."

"Yeah and that's one of 'em."

McArthur took a piece of ham from the table that had been roughly laid to feed the hungry men and poked it into his mouth.

"When's he last had a feed?"

"Last night," Simms remarked.

"Hmm," McArthur went outside into an adjoining cabin. He pushed open a door to where a side of beef hung. He took down the beef and marked off a large piece from the hind leg. He then went back into the cabin where Treeves, Grey and Simms were seated, strode across to the table and tore a large piece of bread off a loaf that sat in the middle of the table. He then took a jug of milk from a nearby cupboard, a platter from in front of Simms, and went out to where Blazer was sitting. When Blazer saw McArthur coming laden with scents that meant food he jumped up and wagged his tail excitedly. McArthur broke the bread and threw a few pieces to Blazer who wolfed them down.

"There's a boy. Here get this down yer," McArthur threw the large chunk of meat uncut in front of the dog. Blazer sniffed it, stood still and then gently put his jaws around it and carried it to the end of the yard farthest away from McArthur. McArthur looked at Blazer as he tilted his head to one side and chewed on the meat severing a piece and gulping it down. He noticed the scar on the underside of the dog, the chewed ear and the tough scarred head, the well muscled and strong squat body.

He thought to himself.

"Hmm, no doubt yer a strong dog, that's for sure, but we'd be giving away too much, every pound of that cur is muscle. But boy, would I love to give Fenton and his brute a taste of their own medicine."

Treeves had come out of the cabin and the two men watched Blazer as he finished off the last of the meat.

"Well, what do yer reckon to him?" Treeves asked.

"Ain't no tellin' just by lookin'. I reckon he'd be up against too much weight and he ain't at his best neither. It would take about three months to get him up to it."

"Well, we got time; we could leave the dog with you."

"Now wait a minute. I didn't say I'd train him."

Blazer had finished the meat and approached the two men wagging his tail and licking his lips. He jumped up at Treeves.

"Git down boy, down," Treeves patted the hard head.

"Sure got a head like a rock, ain't yer, fella."

Treeves hesitated. "Yer see we was thinkin', Simms and Grey and me, that you could—well you'd help us out like, with, well a few dollars, to go up against one of Fenton's dogs."

"What?" McArthur turned and gaped at Treeves. "You must be crazy—yer drag some dog you find up here over one hundred miles and then expect me to stake you."

"I know you're thinking I'd try anything to get at Fenton—sure I'd like to see Fenton's dog beat, but I ain't taking no chance of losing money as well."

"I'm sorry, Treeves, ain't no go." Treeves looked at Blazer.

"But say he beats Fenton's mutt."

"Say he don't," McArthur remarked and turned to go into the cabin.

"Is that yer final word on it?"

"Guess so."

Treeves raised his eyebrows and sighed. "Okay, then if that's how yer feel. Guess we'll just have to enter him on our own 'cos I'm damned sure that even if it means a chance I ain't dragged him all this way just to turn round and go back. I'll see Fenton and see what odds he's got. I've got 50 bucks. It ain't much but I'll stake it."

"Well it's yer money," McArthur replied.

"Yer right—it is and thanks for nothing."

The two men returned to the cabin. Simms and Grey were lighting up a cigarette between them. Simms caught Treeves' look and turned to Grey. Grey shrugged.

"McArthur ain't interested," Treeves remarked.

"Guess we can see that," Grey said as he pulled on the badly rolled cigarette and handed it to Simms.

"Well, now what do we do? Guess we've come this danged far for nothing."

"We still go through with it. I've got fifty bucks, I'll stake him."

"Wait a minute, Treeves, that fifty dollars yer gonna throw around don't happen to belong to you, that happens to be Simms' and mine."

Treeves thought about it for a few minutes, "Okay, then if that's the way you feel about, it take yer fifty dollars and I quit."

Treeves dug into his pocket and pulled out a bunch of screwed up dirty notes and tossed them on to the table in front of Simms and Grey.

"There's yer money."

A fly darted from the table as the notes fluttered on the surface.

Simms and Grey looked at the notes and Grey reached out and grabbed the money in his fist.

"Hmm. Reckon we's quits now as far as the fifty dollars goes," Grey mumbled.

"Reckon we are."

"McArthur, can I bed down somewhere for the night?" Treeves inquired.

"Sure, through there," McArthur nodded to a door which led into a back room.

"I'll put the dog in the barn if that's all right with you. Where does your dog sleep?"

"He usually wanders. I'd better come with you otherwise he might take the seat o' yer pants out walkin' about right an' all."

The two men left the cabin leaving Simms and Grey alone.

"What we gonna do then, Grey?"

Grey thought for a minute "We don't know nothing about dog fightin', McArthur does and he don't reckon the dog's got a chance, so maybe we ought to listen to what he says."

"On the other hand we came a long way just to find that out. We get money though and we get the reward when we take the mutt back," Simms said.

"The thought of that journey don't exactly fill me with pleasure," Grey remarked.

"Perhaps we should do as Treeves reckons and let him fight. If he loses we take him back to Campbell."

"Let's sleep on it. Don't reckon Treeves'll mind if we kip down with him in that room, do yer?"

McArthur and Treeves re-entered the cabin while Blazer settled himself down in the barn raising his head occasionally to bark at some strange nocturnal sound that penetrated the blackness.

Chapter 7

McArthur was up at dawn and had already tidied up the cabin, had breakfast and opened up for trading before any of the three men stirred.

Blazer was barking at a chicken that was strutting about a few yards from where he was tethered, which woke Simms.

The trade that McArthur enjoyed could never at the best of times be called brisk although a few people living a few miles out bought several months' supplies at one time, which usually helped him considerably.

McArthur's place was in a small town where most people knew each other, or of each other, and generally about one another's affairs and who hadn't been to church lately. McArthur had started the store some ten years earlier with his wife, who had died since then. He had carried on as best he could and although his placed lacked a woman's touch he was generally quite a well organized man and reasonably tidy. Local amusement was rather limited and although not as popular as it used to be, a good scrap would be talked about by the menfolk for many a month as much perhaps as the visit of one of the current Boston entertainers hired by the townspeople to perform at the local hall. Most of the fights were held at the town show and fair, when people congregated to display and sell their produce along with apple pie baking contests and tossing a horse shoe over a stake. Also fist fights were a popular spectator sport where the local pugilist would take on all comers.

The day of this summer's fair was set for one week hence and posters had been put up several months before to advertise it.

The two men, Grey and Simms, had decided to enter the dog and had pacified the disgruntled Treeves by offering him a percentage of any winnings. McArthur had said the three men could stay in the barn until the fair was over, and then find alternative accommodations.

During the week preceding the fair, Blazer was fed a good sized portion of meat each day and McArthur had given them some advice on how to bring a dog up to scratch and also instructed them on procedure and rules. In only a week Blazer had responded well to the food and exercise. He weighed about 46 pounds; perhaps four pounds over but it was hardly noticeable. His chain weight could have been anything up to sixty but his fighting weight should have been about forty two. His ribs could clearly be seen and his body was well muscled, the scars on the underside of his belly looked like strips and his lopped ear gave his large head a slightly unbalanced look.

On the day of the fair it was an unusual sight to see three men wandering through the crowds with a tousled white dog on the end of a piece of rope. Blazer took in the crowds without as much as a second glance; one thing he was not afraid of was people but whenever he saw another dog, his head went forward and his body stiffened, straining against the rope.

"Come 'ere—you'll get a chance," Simms jerked on the lead, "yer mangy cur."

It was while they were standing at the barrel where several kids were gathered bobbing for apples in a few feet of water by using just their teeth that Simms noticed a man standing by the arena where the local pugilist was meting out punishment to his opponent—a tall blond boy. The man was staring at Blazer; a puzzled look crossed his face.

"Sean O'Hara." The man in the center of the arena called out the name O'Hara again. Sean swung 'round and stepped up into the arena. He glanced back at the three men and the dog. The noise of the crowd increased and Sean's attention was brought back to the situation in hand.

The blonde boy was being helped from his corner, his face rather bloodied although the crowd applauded as he left the area.

Sean hardly took any notice of the boy. He looked across at his opponent—a balding swarthy unshaven man with a rather fat body, his paunch protruding over the tops of his trousers. The man spat onto each of his hands and rubbed the saliva in. He glared across at Sean and gave an evil grin. Sean cracked his knuckles and took his shirt off; he could hear voices behind him and talk of money and bets. The voice of the referee bellowed above the crowd. The spectators were mainly men but a few children darted around the ring.

The referee announced the contest, brought the two men together and mumbled a few don'ts at them. It cost each man five dollars to enter and if they lasted three rounds they got fifty dollars. No one as yet had gone the three rounds. Sean's opponent grinned again. Sean winced visibly as the man's breath assailed his nostrils.

"Yer breath stinks," Sean remarked to the man.

The man growled back, "You won't even be able to smell smellin' salts by the time I've finished with you."

The referee pushed the two men apart and the fight began. The signal for the round to end was the sound of a pan being struck repeatedly with a stick. The fighter strode across the ring and swung a vicious left. The huge fist made the air sing as Sean ducked out of the way. Sean counterattacked instantly with a short right and left to the man's belly and stepped back. The crowd cheered as the sound of large amounts of flesh being smacked hard reached their ears. The fighter seemed surprised but not hurt; he stepped forward and lashed out with his right at the bobbing head of the Irishman.

"Stay still, yer little rat."

"Oh, sure, so's yer can hit me."

The Irishman had already decided that in no way could he outpunch this man toe to toe. His only

At the fair

chance was to stay out of the way and wear him down. Again the Irishman thudded a powerful jab into the paunch of the fighter. Sean turned deftly as the man, becoming more enraged, rushed at him; he turned sideways and delivered a snap punch to the man's temple. This had a visible effect on the fighter; he reeled and tottered under the blow. Sean unleashed two more blows at the reeling head. The crowd cheered and waved excitedly. The fighter's promoter from the corner shuffled uneasily and bellowed at his swarthy protegé who was still dazedly searching for the elusive Irishman.

Two large bruises had appeared on the unshaven face; the man was also breathing heavily. Sean took up a pugilistic stance and came closer to the fighter. Through the blur the man saw the shape of the Irishman advancing with his fists raised. He blinked a couple of times and just as he had focused on his adversary, his chin jerked upward under the enormous power of the Irishman's fist; again another blow to the side of his head made his knees go weak and he sank slowly to the floor and crumpled into a large heap of untidy flesh. The promoter spat disgustedly into the ring. Several spectators were already through the ropes clapping the unruffled Irishman heartily on the back as the referee reached the count of ten. Grey, Simms and Treeves had witnessed the fight and were nodding appreciatively.

Simms looked puzzled, "Where have I seen that man before?" he muttered to himself.

"Well wherever it is, let's hope this mutt is as good as him."

"Now where's this second of Fenton's that we're supposed to meet here?" Even as Simms spoke one of the more unpleasant looking spectators watching the fight turned from the crowd and came over to the three men.

"You Treeves?" the man asked.

"Yeah."

"Follow me," the man turned from the three and strode off in the direction of a timbered house. The man's name was Henry Fowler, an associate of Fenton's, who raised and trained his dogs. He was also Fenton's handyman and general dogsbody.

Treeves had been to see Fenton during the week preceding the fair and Fenton had agreed to a match on his terms if that's what the three had wanted but had also added that the match was rather uneven. Fowler also kept a book for Fenton, knowing that whenever he fought his dogs there was always a healthy crowd—meaning quite a few dollars on the side.

The fight was to take place behind one of the fairground stalls. The sheriff had stipulated the usual conditions to Fenton and even the Mayor.

>※※◇※※◇※※◇※※◇※※<

There were already a few people hanging about when Treeves, Simms and Grey appeared with Blazer trotting behind on the end of his rope. A couple of men leaning against a gatepost sniggered as they saw Blazer. Simms caught this and turned to Grey to see if he had noticed this display of confidence. If he had he did not show it but was looking around to see if he could see Fenton.

Fowler halted and approached another equally smart-looking man who glanced at the three men and then walked off into the crowd. Treeves, Grey and Simms looked uneasily about them trying not to feel conspicuous.

"Hmm, where's this other critter then?" Grey asked.

"I don't see Fenton anywhere—wait a minute—this looks like him." Through the crowd a thin weedy looking man was leading a powerful looking dog. It was similar in size to a bull mastiff but its jaws were heavier, its fawn body was well muscled and its ears had been cropped.

Blazer hadn't noticed the presence of the other animal but his nose began to twitch and he lifted his head to allow his nostrils to taste the slight breeze.

"Looks kinda big next to our mutt," Grey remarked.

"Yeah that's him all right," Treeves muttered. He waved across at Fenton. Fenton acknowledged the recognition and lifted his hand in response.

"Well let's git to it. Where's they gonna set to then?" Simms enquired.

"It's just a square that's been drawn and there's a line—it ain't nothing fancy 'cos of the fact of where we are and the conditions under which we are entering him."

The crowd had gathered and already formed a loose square around Fenton's dog. Treeves and the two men pushed their way through the crowd and entered the square. The two dogs now caught sight of each other and both stiffened. Fenton's 'Trojan' strained at the leash and it was as much as Fenton could do to restrain him.

"Here, hold Trojan, Henry," Fenton passed the end of the leash to Fowler and walked across the square to Treeves. As he reached the three men, the familiar figure of McArthur appeared next to the white dog.

"Well, well, are yer here as ref or what? Jebb has agreed to ref this one."

"Suits me, Fenton" answered McArthur.

"I've come here as the dog's handler."

"Well, ain't much point explaining the rules to you," Fenton's mouth curled up in a sarcastic smile.

Jebb got the buckets organized and "You can taste the dog's water if yer like." Fenton turned back and went over to his dog.

Jebb, a Canadian type lumberjack complete with checked shirt and beard shouted at the crowd to keep well back and let the dogs have plenty of room. The crowd sometimes got over enthusiastic and the space the dogs were in got so small that neither dog could get out if it wanted to or maneuver for a better hold.

The usual rituals were observed, Jebb finally explaining the rules to both sides. Fenton won the toss and Trojan was to be the first to scratch. The crowd expectantly waited as the large fawn dog was released, Fenton giving the animal a reassuring pat on the rump as the snarling creature leapt across toward where Blazer stood quivering. Blazer's condition was not tiptop but on the other hand he was not too overweight and reasonably fit. His gameness had in no way diminished. Some people call it downright stupid to go in against all odds without sign of fear and fight to the death. If this quality was

Blazer and Trojan going at it

stupidity then Blazer was indeed a stupid dog. He braced himself for the impact of the 120 lb. mass of aggressive muscle that thundered toward him. McArthur slipped the dog seconds after Fowler released Trojan. The crowd cheered as the two dogs met.

Trojan caught Blazer on the side pushing him 'round rather than knocking the wind out of him. Blazer had sidestepped the animal without even being aware of it and came in hard on the dog's shoulder. The sheer weight of the travelling dog had caused Blazer's grip to fail, not allowing him enough time to get any amount of flesh between his teeth. Trojan swung 'round and caught Blazer by the back of the neck and threw him several feet. The dog had intended to embed his fangs and tear but his grip had not been firm enough (as had not Blazer's) and Blazer had been released, simultaneously being tossed in the air and thrown several feet. Blazer had landed badly and turned around to find his opponent. Obviously a little dazed when he caught sight of the fawn fury, he stood still.

The crowd roared. Jebb shouted to McArthur "Scratch the dog."

Fowler reached out and caught Trojan in mid charge. Blazer rushed at the fawn dog and McArthur stepped forward and caught him as Fowler restrained Trojan. A dog is allowed five seconds to make up its mind; if there is any doubt, then the dogs are scratched. If on the next occasion the dog does the same hesitant performance, then it loses.

Blazer was taken back and faced against Trojan. McArthur released him. The white dog raced across the square formed by the crowd.

"Well, he ain't scared of 'im," Grey remarked to Simms as he watched Blazer race toward Trojan.

"No, but not being scared ain't enough," Treeves muttered.

Chapter 8

A dog that is experienced in the pit survives only if it can defeat its opponent. Also it learns to do this with the minimum discomfort to itself, although in the heat of a scrap it hardly looks as though the animal gives a damn about his own welfare. The dog to survive must also think where to attack with the best results from such an attack. Blazer had fought many opponents and several of them had been larger and stronger. Blazer knew that an opponent had weak spots which would enable him to finish the animal easier. Perhaps in that hesitation Blazer through his daze realized that by sheer brute force he would not defeat this dog. No one can say what goes through a dog's mind, but for all appearances' sake Blazer began a more tactical fight—when he reached the fawn dog he leapt up and came down hard on the animal's back. The larger dog turned and met Blazer as he came down astride him; the powerful jaws of the dog sought a grip to dislodge the white fury. Trojan rolled on his back and his head turned and secured a grip on Blazer's shoulder. Blazer had a mouthful of flesh from the other's neck. The fawn dog's neck muscles heaved as Blazer, with the full weight of his adversary on him, clung tenaciously to his neck. Gradually Blazer was pulled off. Both dogs simultaneously released each other and turned face to face. Trojan, after having sprung to his feet, bored in, the sheer power of the animal pushing the smaller dog back. Blazer's hard head banged against Trojan's and his fangs took hold of the dog's cheek—again the weight of the fawn dog pushed Blazer forward into the crowd. The onlookers parted as the two dogs entered their ranks, the larger dog unable to use his fangs to any advantage, and Blazer gripping the dog's cheek being forced backward through the parting spectators.

Jebb had followed the dogs and at the same time created a path for the struggles. The ground became dusty as the dogs churned up the area. Blazer suddenly released his hold and clamped his teeth firmly on the crossbreed's front who responded by biting into Blazer's neck. The squat body was already taut and the skin fitted tightly over the bulging muscles. The large dog's teeth bit and tore into the white fur without securing a firm hold. Blazer released the foreleg and with lightning speed pulled away from the searching jowls and clamped himself once more on his adversary's cheek. Trojan gave a squeal of pain and his snarls indicated his displeasure at this situation. He was virtually power-less to inflict any damage on Blazer for every time he turned his head Blazer pulled in the opposite direction, restraining him through pain.

Fenton had been watching the fight dispassionately, while on the other side Simms had been almost down on all fours yelling encouragement at Blazer. Grey and Treeves had also lent their voices to the cacophony of sound that emitted from the crowd in favor of Blazer. A man pushed his way through the mob and stood next to the yelling Simms. He looked at the three men and then at the two fighting dogs. The crowd screaming and shouting encouragement. The faces of both men and women engrossed in the canine battle before them. Grey casually glanced at the man and recognized him as the Irishman who had fought in the ring earlier.

The dogs had been at it now for about ten minutes and Fenton was surprised that this little dog had lasted so long. Trojan usually had no trouble with smaller dogs, his large powerful jaws securing a grip and finishing it in the first few minutes, but this little white un was fighting the dog on his own terms, securing a grip, inflicting damage to the dog's foreleg and then with lightning speed taking hold of Trojan's cheek before the dog had time to recover. Although not the most agile of dogs, Blazer by comparison to Trojan was a gymnast.

One of the reasons that fighting dogs were bred smaller was because the bigger dogs proved cumbersome and heavy in the pit, the smaller dogs proving equally as game but the added agility made them more suitable for combat and also from the spectators' point of view. While Sean took in the scene Blazer continued to release, hack at Trojan's foreleg and then secure a grip. Trojan, as soon as Blazer released, jerked his head back out of the way of Blazer's fangs. Blazer sensing that he would not be able to take hold instantly bit hard upon the animal's leg and swung his head away from the dog's jaws. Trojan, enraged by the pain and now with his head free, bore into Blazer's exposed shoulder. The steel jaws clamped down hard. Blazer tore and bit with all his force on the leg. A spurt of blood came from the side of his mouth. Fenton cursed and swore at what he saw.

McArthur grinned across at him. Jebb turned towards Fowler. Fenton nodded and Fowler stepped across, waved to McArthur and the two men went in to separate the dogs. The crowd jeered. "Let 'em finish it," a woman screamed. "Take him out," Fenton spoke above the crowd.

Trojan was pried off Blazer and looked slightly bewildered as he was taken back to his corner. Blazer licked the blood from his jaws and wagged his tail as McArthur patted the scarred head. All in all Blazer had come through reasonably unscathed. Trojan's last grip could have proven difficult for the dog—but Blazer had seemingly taken his chance in order to inflict his own damage.

Trojan, on the other hand, had blood coming from his cheek although this would quickly heal. What had caused Fenton to pull his dog out was that Blazer had severed a main artery. With the activity of the fight Trojan would soon have lost too much blood, become weak and eventually lost, even died, although Fenton was at one point considering letting him continue because of the grip he now had. It was a case of who would crack first and knowing dogs as he did he decided not to take the chance.

McArthur pushed his way through the crowd which was now dispersing, disappointed at not seeing more blood and 'sport'. Although Fenton's dog had never been beaten and the bookkeepers cleaned up, Fenton had not lost financially; he always covered himself with the Book and Trojan would live to fight another day.

"Perhaps you'd like to try yer dog again" Fenton said to McArthur.

"Perhaps."

"Perhaps not."

Both men turned toward the voice. It was Sean who had followed McArthur across the ring.

"And why not?" enquired McArthur, recognizing the Irishman as the one he saw in the ring, the sight of the large swarthy fighter buckling under Sean's fist coming clearly into his mind's eye as he said it.

"Cos de dog ain't yours to fight."

"That dog belongs to a Mr. Treeves and his two partners."

"Where did they get him?" Sean asked.

"They found him about 100 miles south of here."

"I suppose he was just wandering about."

"He was."

"Well if dat's de case I'll return him to his owner, a Mr. Campbell who has been looking for him for some considerable time."

Simms and Grey leading Blazer approached the men.

"Hey lookee here," Simms held up $200. "Looks like we got us a winner."

Treeves came up behind.

It was Simms who recognized Sean first and quickly nudged Grey. Grey reacted to the sharp elbow in his ribs by first letting out a gasp as the blow winded him and then an angry shout.

"Hey what's with you?"

Again Simms nudged Grey and nodded his head toward the Irishman.

"It's that Irishman," Simms whispered.

"Yeah I know, the one in the ring."

"Yeah but he's the one who was asking about the dog, that time. I thought I'd seen him before."

Grey registered an expression of recognition.

"Yeah, yeah, you're right, what the hell's he doing here?"

McArthur turned around and beckoned Grey and Simms who were now beginning to head in the opposite direction.

"Hey, Simms, Grey," McArthur called out.

Treeves had wandered up to where Sean and McArthur stood.

"What's up?"

"This gentleman says that this dog 'Blazer' he calls him, don't belong to you."

"Why not?" Treeves enquired, suddenly recognizing Sean from the fight Blazer had with the wolf.

"He says that the dog belongs to a Mr. Campbell and that this Campbell brought the dog from England last November and that he got out one night and ain't been seen since."

120

Grey and Simms came over to McArthur realizing that no way could they make a run for it, and besides there was no way of proving they had stolen the dog, also that in fact the dog had actually approached them. Sean turned towards the two men and Blazer.

"Hey Blazer, come here, boy."

Blazer wagged his tail and sniffed his nose, licking Sean's face and nipping the Irishman's ears.

Sean stood up.

"Seems like I remember asking you two about this dog some time ago."

"Well, yeah, of course, I remember it. Is this the dog?" Grey remarked "Well that is lucky. That means we got the reward."

"Yeah what was it, about $200?" Simms remarked.

"Mr. Campbell offered that reward but it seems like you had no intention of taking the dog back."

"Of course we did. We just happen to be around here with the dog and then we were heading back to Boston."

"Well I'll save you the journey. I'll take the dog back." Sean reached across and snatched the end of the rope from Simms.

"Wait a minute," Treeves interrupted."You can't just come along and take this dog, you ain't got no proof that you are going to take him back. How do we know you ain't just going off somewhere?"

Sean turned towards Treeves, "You don't."

"Anyways," continued Treeves, "what are you doing up here if you work for Campbell, why ain't yer back there?"

In truth Sean had left Campbell's employ just after Blazer had run off, feeling responsible for the loss of the dog. He had tried in vain to find him. It was by pure coincidence that he had been here at this time. It was his plan to go as far north as possible and then if things became hard to head back to New York and take a job in the city. Now having found Blazer at least he could return to Campbell and perhaps take up his old position.

"I've come this far looking for the dog," Sean replied.

Grey and Simms both doubted this but neither of them had the courage to say outright that they thought this was slightly untruthful. Not one of the three wished to take on the Irishman after having just witnessed his performance in the ring. Simms mentally winced as his imagination momentarily took over and presented him with a picture of his own chin jerking violently back and his teeth going in all directions.

"Well now, let's talk this out," Simms remarked.

"Perhaps then you can give us the reward on behalf of this Mr. Campbell, seeing as you is acting as his agent so to speak."

Grey nodded appreciatively, slightly surprised at the sense of Simms' statement.

Treeves thought for a moment; he didn't really have any passionate desire to fight dogs and besides he had made a few dollars extra and kept his fifty. He also wouldn't want to take on this man purely to defend Grey and Simms, who were old enough and certainly ugly enough to fight their own battles. He stroked his large red beard.

"Hmm. Reckon that don't seem a bad idea seeing as you are acting as Mr. Campbell's agent."

"I've got $150 on me; you can either take that or come back to Campbell's spread and collect the full $200. Take it or leave it." The three men went a few yards away from Sean and muttered together.

"What have we got to lose," Grey argued, "just cos he beat this mutt don't mean to say he's gonna win the next and besides it's too much bother looking after him what with feedin' and all and $150 is better than nothing."

"I kinda like him," Simms said.

"I know I don't have as much say as you two but I reckon Grey's right. If we refuse, we'll have to take on this Irishman. I reckon the three of us could do it but is it worth the sweat? I say you should take the $150."

The three men returned to Sean.

"Okay, Mister, we'll take the $150," Grey stated.

Sean reached into his pocket and took out the money.

"Here," he reached across and Grey took it.

"Better count it," Simms put in.

"Yeah." Grey laboriously thumbed his way through the notes finally concluding that all was correct.

Fenton had been watching the proceedings and now addressed Sean.

"Do you want to sell him?" he asked.

"How much?" Sean asked.

The three men's eyebrows raised and Treeves' jaw dropped.

Fenton put his head to one side and thought, his teeth bit into his lower lip.

"Well, about four hundred dollars seems a reasonable amount."

Simms could not hold back his indignation, "Now come on, Fenton, what's the game?"

Sean smiled, "I'm sorry Mister, he ain't mine to sell."

Sean turned and led the dog away.

Chapter 9

The weather was still warm and the nights balmy apart from the odd shower that Sean might experience so he could sleep comfortably outside. Not that the journey would take him long; he had a good horse and Blazer could keep going, his wounds were negligible, and wouldn't slow him down. Sean didn't want to waste any time; he left the fair after eating his fill of a large apple pie he bought from one of the stalls and also a pot of honey which was his favorite. For the dog he bought a large piece of cow beef which the yard man cut up into several hunks and some ammunition to try and shoot some fresh meat. Sean bagged this up and slung it across the back of his horse. He also bought a small pan which cost him his last fifty cents.

Sean had been surprised at the reaction of Blazer to the horse. After barking a few times at the animal Blazer had sneezed violently and turned away with distinterest.

"Well, looks like you've learned some sense in yer old age," Sean remarked. He mounted the horse and after having lengthened the rope led the dog after him. Blazer followed. The two set off, leaving the small town and the fair still in full swing. The festivities would continue well into the evening finishing with a dance. Sean smiled at the very thought of it.

"And here I am saddled with a smelly white dog—something's gotta be wrong somewhere, Lord."

Sean dug his heels into the side of the horse and urged him on.

"Let's get going. The sooner we get back the better."

After a few miles out Sean released the dog and watched to see what he'd do. Blazer did nothing. He stood still waiting for Sean to move.

"Well, I don't reckon you'll run away after all. Where are you going to run to? Certainly not back to those three. Blazer, me lad, I don't know what you can see keeping such company indeed." A rabbit bobbed out from behind a rock several yards ahead.

"Now be holding still, will yer Blazer." Sean reached slowly down to his rifle and gently eased it out of its case. He loaded it as silently as he could and raised it to his shoulder. Blazer raised his head and caught sight of the rabbit. He growled then gave out a pathetic yelp and rushed toward the rabbit.

"Hold it, Blazer!" Sean took quick aim at the rabbit which was now standing on its hind legs, ears erect, and pulled the trigger. The rabbit dropped down on all fours at the same time the bullet whistled over its head. Blazer had heard gunfire before and usually associated it with something to eat, lying around immediately afterwards. He continued to chase the rabbit which by now had leapt off behind the rock from where it came.

"Blast you, Blazer, yer stupid dog. Yer nearly got yerself shot and yer lost yer dinner and fighting dogs are supposed to be intelligent." Sean spurred the horse toward the rock where both dog and rabbit had disappeared.

Blazer was sniffing excitedly around the base of the rock occasionally jumping on all fours giving the appearance of a frisky lamb. Sean laughed out loud.

"You silly creature, you think he's gonna hang around for you to grab him. Come on, let's bed down here and get some grub organized."

Sean unpacked his bed roll and collected some wood to make a fire. It was getting toward dusk and the mosquitoes were beginning to bite. Blazer went scurrying off in a patch of briar nearby searching for rabbits while Sean brewed some coffee.

"Don't think I can handle any grub. I can still taste that apple pie," he said to Blazer as the dog briefly popped his head up and then continued his search in the bracken.

"Ain't yer hungry?" Sean enquired of the dog who looked at him, a scratch clearly visible on his nose.

Blazer came bounding over toward the Irishman, racing past him and then rushing back again, his tail tucked between his legs running around and around in circles brushing next to Sean, stopping to look at the man and then racing off again.

"You have a good run, go on then," Sean ran after the dog. Blazer raced off twisting 'round and 'round and then scudding away. Eventually he stopped and lay panting on the grass, his back legs straight out behind. He dragged his body forward with his front legs across the grass, his head looking for all intents and purposes as if he had a broad grin on his face.

"Lordy me, Saints preserve us. I've got better things to do than chase you around. Let's get you some grub."

It took Sean four days to get back to Campbell's place. As he entered the familiar yard he dropped from the horse's back and slipped the rope around Blazer's neck.

Mrs. Fiona Campbell was talking to a woman and a little girl as Sean appeared.

"Sean. Excuse me, Mrs. Arnot." Mrs. Campbell stepped from the porch and went over to the Irishman.

"Sean, how are you? How good to see you. Ian's in the house; do come in."

The little girl ran down from her mother's side and went over to the dog.

"Mary, come here—don't touch that dog."

"He's all right, mummy—I know Blazer." Mary Arnot flung her arms around the dog's neck.

Blazer wagged his tail furiously and snorted and snuffled knocking the little girl's parasol from her

Blazer and Mary playing together

hand. Blazer snatched up the parasol and shook it furiously.

"Hey," Sean took the end of the parasol, "Let go—come on."

Blazer stood still, his eyes firmly fixed on Sean, his tail wagging.

"It's all right, Sean. I know he's only playing," the little girl said.

"Come on, Blazer, don't be naughty."

Blazer let go of the parasol and barked up at Mary.

"I'm sorry about that, Mrs. Arnot, and good day, Mrs. Campbell. I'll just have a word with Mr. Campbell. I'll just take the dog to the barn."

"Oh, let me hold him, Sean," Mary pleaded.

"Well er, if that's all right with yer mother."

"That's okay, Sean," Mrs. Arnot nodded.

"Now you hold tight, Mary—throw a stick for him, he likes dat."

Sean tousled Mary's hair and went up the steps into the house. He entered the hallway, conscious of his dusty feet. Campbell's butler greeted him.

"Mr. O'Hara—How are you? Mr. Campbell is in the study."

The butler showed Sean through the beautiful interior to a large oak door where he knocked and waited. A voice bade him enter. He opened the door for Sean and waved him on.

Campbell was seated at a large wooden desk near the window of a wood-paneled room which looked out across green lawns and a sizeable pond. He rose as he saw Sean.

"Well, well, the prodigal returns."

"Beg pardon, sir?" Sean asked.

"Sean, what are you doing here? We thought you were living it up in New York?"

"Well sir, I was on me way there when I happened to stop by at the summer fair and then while I was enjoying the town's hospitality so to speak, I happened to see a dog which will be familiar to you, sir."

"Blazer!" Campbell interrupted.

"Yes sir, the very same."

"Well what happened. Did you —"

"Yes sir, I've got him with me."

"How is he?"

"Well sir, one could say fightin' fit. He was sorting out this big half breed giving away twice his weight."

"Where is he then, Sean?"

"Outside sir, playing with young Mary Arnot."

Campbell went out of the study to the front of the house, Sean following. The two men went out into the sunshine. Fiona Campbell and Mrs. Arnot were still talking while Mary had one end of a stick on which Blazer was tugging. The dog could easily have pulled the little girl along the ground, but whenever he gained what he thought was sufficient ground he'd stop and let Mary pull him the other way, all the while growling fiercely.

"Hey Blazer—Blazer, here boy."

Blazer's eyes moved to the direction of the sound but his grip on the stick remained. Campbell and Sean went to the dog.

"I'm sorry to interrupt your game, Mary, but can I just have a look at Blazer? He's been away a long time, as you know. I just want to see if he's fit and well."

"Here, Mr. Campbell, you take the stick then."
Mary handed the stick to Campbell. Blazer clung to
the other end. Campbell drew the stick closer to
him.

"Come here, you silly dog."

Campbell examined the dog as Blazer growled
and pulled against the resistance of the man's
hand. Campbell patted Blazer and released the
stick. The dog trotted off jauntily with the stick in
his mouth. "Okay Mary love, he looks all right to me;
you can play now."

Mary ran after Blazer who ambled off just keeping
ahead of her.

"Well Mr. Campbell, what do you reckon?"

"Just after you left, Sean, Rearden came over to
see me. Evidently he found Blazer clinging to the
throat of some cat that had escaped from some
settlers' place and had been killing sheep. Arnot's
dog was with him but was killed. I reckon that's who
Blazer took off with that night."

"He must have been pretty badly cut up taking on
a cat."

"Yeah, that's where he got those neat rows of
stripes underneath him."

"Well, how come he got so far north?"

"Rearden said that two men, Simms and Grey,
took him, stole him that is; he was quite surprised
that the dog wasn't here when he arrived. He
thought they were after the reward."

"I see," Sean mused, "I asked dem no goods
soon after the dog was gone; they said they knew
nothing about it."

"They probably didn't then. Anyway how did you
get him from them?"

"I just took him," Sean replied.

"Come Sean, I know you're a hard man to beat but two men?"

"There was four in all—but we came to an arrangement, so to speak."

"Well, you must accept the reward then," Campbell suggested.

"Not on yer life, sir; I felt responsible for the loss of the dog and now he's back—that's squared it. If yer still have a job for me,sir, I'd like to be working for you again, sir. I reckon there's still that redbrick Willie to be taken care of."

Campbell clapped Sean on his broad shoulders.

"Welcome back, Mr. O'Hara, and pleased I am to have you here. Let's just have a little nip to celebrate the event."

Sean visibly brightened at the thought.

"Now I think I can be persuaded, sir, to accommodate you."

The two men chuckled and turned back toward the house. Campbell was pleased to have both Sean and Blazer back and in the following weeks saw the improvement in the dog's health. His coat took on a sheen and the muscled lean body stood out under the fur when he moved.

Chapter 10

It was one evening in September that Campbell crossed the drive to the barn where Blazer slept. Sean was cleaning some tool as Campbell entered. Blazer jumped up and walked to the end of his chain, his tail wagging. Campbell patted the scarred head.

"Hello, Blazer. I've just seen Brady, Sean; He's agreed for two weeks from next Saturday a few miles out of town in Spencer's barn. Brady has upped the wager to $4000."

Sean let out a low whistle.

"Is it worth it, Mr. Campbell, sir? I mean you're talking about a lot of money."

"It's not the money, Sean. I've already spent far more than a lot of people think the dog's worth. It's not that; Brady thinks he owns the top dog and I know I do or at least I'm pretty sure."

"Well, whatever, it would be some fight."

"It promises to be quite an evening. Spencer has engaged a couple of singers and will be offering refreshment before the dogs go on."

Sean smiled and patted Blazer. "I've been at him quite a bit lately; if ever he was in tip top condition it's now. Oh there's just one thing, sir. Arnot's little girl. She comes with her mother quite a lot and makes a bee line for the dog. It might be a bit upsetting for her if she saw him just after a scrap."

Campbell thought for a minute.

"Yeah, maybe you're right. I'll speak to Fiona and see if we can arrange it that the dog is out of the way for some reason. Thanks, Sean."

※※◇※※◇※※◇※※

The October air had a distinct chill in it as Sean and Campbell and the dog arrived at the Spencer place. They were both a little early and Campbell jumped down from the buckboard and knocked at the door. A flap on the door opened and a face peered out. On recognizing Campbell the door was opened.

"Good evening, Mr. Campbell. Come in." Spencer was the owner of the place and a converted barn which he used as a workshop and plant shed. Several crates of liquor were piled up in the corner and a few rounds of cheese were stacked next to them. A piano stood near to the door.

"You're early, Mr. Campbell," Spencer said.

"Yes, we didn't know how long it would take us and I want the dog to get warm first."

Several people were milling about arranging seating.

"What will happen, Mr. Campbell, is that first the

singers will start off. Then McAddum has got two cocks he wants to set down; then the main event."

Campbell nodded.

"Bring your man in and have a drink; it's too cold for standing around."

Spencer broke off and shouted across to a man who was sweeping an area of the floor.

"Hey, George keep the dust down—and there are some benches against the house you can use."

A few more people drifted in. Spencer called across to a large bearded man. "Hey, Joe, get on the door will you—check out a few faces."

The man moved and stood by the door.

"I'll fetch Sean and the dog," Campbell said.

"Right, Mr. Campbell."

Campbell went out to get Sean, noting as he went the difference in the way a barn can look after a little re-arrangement and sweeping. It gave him an idea for his own barn. The trouble was that as a 'respectable' citizen it would hardly do him good if his premises were the subject of a raid and he were found to be conducting illegal activities on his property.

"Hey Sean, take the buckboard 'round the side. I'll take Blazer."

"Right, Mr. Campbell," Sean tugged at Blazer's rope and Blazer jumped down from the wagon. Campbell grabbed the end of the rope and led the dog inside into the relative warmth of the barn-cum-auditorium.

Blazer was alert. He knew what the activity meant. The smells and sounds of people. To him a crowd meant only one association—a fight. His body

136

trembled slightly; he was like a coiled spring ready for action.

Campbell approached Spencer.

"You haven't got a back room somewheres that I can keep the dog? I don't want him getting all riled up before he goes in, what with cock fighting and all that commotion."

"Certainly, Mr. Campbell."

"Hey George, show Mr. Campbell to the house and put him in Betty's room."

George nodded and leaned his broom against the barn wall.

"This way, sir."

"Thanks, Spencer," Campbell said and followed the shape ahead of him.

They crossed from the barn to Spencer's house. George knocked on the door and Mrs. Spencer opened it.

"Jim says Mr. Campbell can stay here for a while."

Mrs. Spencer looked at Campbell and the dog.

"Come in, Mr. Campbell," Meg Spencer nodded her head. "Thanks, George."

"I hope I'm not putting you to any trouble, Meg."

"No, no, it's all right, come in and make yourself at home." She led Campbell into the small front room. Blazer tugged on the end of the rope.

"This way, Blazer." Campbell yanked the dog back.

"Would you like some coffee, Mr. Campbell?" Meg asked.

"Oh, no thanks, Meg. I'll just sit if I may. Quite a busy evening your husband's got going for himself."

Meg nodded; she looked at Blazer, "Is that the dog everyone's talking about?"

"I suppose so Meg, yes."

"With due respect, Mr. Campbell, I think it's a mighty cruel pasttime; I can't see how it can be Christian to watch creatures fight one another for fun."

"Well, it's hardly for fun, Meg; there's quite a lot of money involved."

"I'm ashamed of Jim for his part and I've told him so."

"I can believe you have, Meg."

Campbell reached down and pressed Blazer's hindquarters, "Down! Blazer." Getting the dog to keep still was quite an effort, let alone make him sit down.

"Well, if you'll excuse me, Mr. Campbell I've got a few chores to attend to."

"Of course, Meg, and thank you."

Meg bobbed out of the room and Campbell was left alone.

Blazer whimpered and looked up at Campbell.

"All right, in a minute you'll get your go, in a minute."

The man sat back in the chair and his thoughts dwelt on what Meg had just said. He imagined the slim woman verbally attacking her husband and Spencer pacifying her with a few "yes dears" while stacking up the crates of alcohol. "I suppose she was right; it hardly seemed a Christian-like thing to do." He imagined the twelve Apostles gathered round the edge of the pit in their long robes egging two combatants on—Campbell smiled. "Hardly" he muttered aloud. Blazer's ears pricked up.

"It's all right, Blaze," the dog flopped to the floor with a sigh, obviously resigned to the fact that not a lot was going to happen in this room.

"I don't know, boy." Campbell had often thought about his role in dog fighting and although he undeniably got pleasure from seeing the dogs fight, somewhere at the back of his mind a pang of conscience would often creep in. He dismissed it with a shrug. "Well, here we are, and there's a lot of money riding on your ability, Blazer," he addressed the dog.

From the barn things had begun to warm up and the sound of a piano drifted across to the house. Blazer's stubby ear pricked up and he gave a little bark.

"Won't be long, Blaze. We'll give it a few more minutes and then take a stroll."

Chapter 11

Back at the barn the air hung heavy with tobacco smoke and it looked like the local stag party in full swing. The audience consisted mostly of men, some well dressed, but the majority casually attired in overalls and shirts. An old man was hammering on the piano and two rather older than younger women decked out in feathery costumes were rendering an old music hall number to their best ability. The act finished amid tumultuous applause and cat calls.

Spencer smiled appreciatively and nodded to George who promptly disappeared behind a screen at the far end of the barn. Two men appeared, each with a fowl under his arm and talking heatedly to each other.

Spencer ushered the spectators into a rough circle and George produced some chalk and drew a line. The crowd was in good humor after the girls' song, and wagers were taken on the outcome of the scrap. The feathered foes were placed opposite each other and held a few inches apart. Neither of them wore spurs although their natural weaponry had been utilized as much as possible. Each fowl as it was held by its owner clucked and struggled to get at the opponent. Both handlers knelt down facing each other and placed the birds within a circle which George had drawn. A man acting as the referee exchanged a few words with the owners and then the birds were released. The large antagonist, a black speckled bird with a bright comb, strutted forward hopping and ducking, using his beak and rapidly pecking the smaller brown bird as it strutted equally as arrogantly in an effort to use its feet. The onslaught of the speckled bird proved all too daunting for the brown cock who gave out a loud cluck, turned and sprung onto the shoulder of one of the spectators. Using the startled man's anatomy as a lever, it leapt nimbly across the heads of the mob, avoiding the odd outstretched hand grasping in an effort to restrain its advance. The bird ducked and flapped its way around the confines of the barn, finally coming to rest in one of the rafters, the disgruntled owner standing beneath it screaming abuse. The crowd seemed to enjoy this spectacle as much as the promised sport, cheering and shouting. Eventually the speckled cock was declared the winner by default and the brown bird was left roosting in the rafters until later when it could be retrieved.

Spencer with two assistants came through the rear of the barn with a large square wooden structure. It was the walls of a makeshift arena in which the dogs were to fight. He pushed and maneuvered his way through the spectators and with the aid of the two men erected it in the center of the barn.

"George, push the piano further back."

"Where's Brady?" Spencer looked around trying to see if he could catch a glimpse among the many faces.

"Henry, get the buckets and towels and bring some more chalk. Oh and tell Mr. Campbell to come across; no, don't bother; he's here."

Campbell had come in and was standing with Sean. Blazer was raring to go and his beady eyes were searching for his opponent.

"Ah, there's Brady," Sean noted.

Brady had been standing outside with his dogs and was now talking to a couple of his men.

"Hang on to Blazer, Sean. I'll just go and sort out the financial side with Brady."

Campbell shouldered his way across the barn.

"Ah, Mr. Campbell," Brady shook Campbell's hand.

"Evening, Brady—Hi boy!" Campbell reached down and stroked the red colored dog. He noted the square look of the animal, the large size for the weight, the long heavily muscled neck, ideal in a fighting dog, enabling him to reach vital parts in a hold—the broad hips meaning a lot of muscle at the rear end, the well bent back and the deep rib cage indicating the large lung capacity. The size of the head powerful but not over large, with the lips not getting in the way of his canines.

"Nice dog, Brady."

"Thank you, Mr. Campbell. Shall we deposit our funds with Spencer? After you, Mr. Campbell."

Brady handed the dog to his man and the two men went in search of Spencer. Both had agreed on four thousand dollars as the prize money and each deposited their purses with Spencer who put it in his safe and posted an armed man within easy reach. A lot of money was at stake this evening; several businessmen were among the crowd and the bookies were busy. Campbell noted the Mayor and a few local dignitaries vying for a favorable position among the heads.

"Well, at least we won't be disturbed," he thought to himself.

The crowd finally settled down into some form of orderly viewing arrangement and expectancy of a good scrap ran high as the dogs were washed and dried. A couple of dishes of water were brought in for the animals should they need it.

The referee, Altoll, the German who had officiated at Blazer's last fight spoke to Sean and then to Brady's handler. Brady and Campbell positioned themselves immediately outside the wooden enclosure. Brady won the toss and Redbrick was the first to scratch. Blazer had been eyeing his opponent and knew the time had arrived to realize his ambitions to sink his teeth into the other animal. The dogs met head on, Sean releasing Blazer seconds after the hands of Brady's man let go of the struggling dog. Both dogs went in low and started to wrestle, each feeling the other out, both experienced fighters. Blazer took the first hold on Red's front leg and Red pushed and leaned forward to take hold of Blazer's stifle, the length of his neck enabling him to reach under Blazer. Blazer sensing and feeling the fangs closing around him released the foreleg and jumped clear. Redbrick could have caused considerable damage. Campbell moaned a sigh of relief. Thank God he's wise to that one now, he thought. Red bored in for the attack; he clamped on to Blazer's nose and shook it vigorously. Blazer gave a yelp of pain and pushed forward following the dog in order not to resist the pressure. Red shook again, his powerful neck muscles clearly visible. Again Blazer yelped. Campbell sympathized with the dog and his hand involuntarily went to his nose. Red released his hold on Blazer and took his ear. Blazer's nose visibly torn and bleeding, again Red shook vigorously. Blazer turned to try and secure a grip on his antagonist but could not pull against the dog's hold. Again Red released the ear and tried for a cheek hold; both dogs grappled and stood on their hind legs, the larger red standing fractionally higher than Blazer, forcing him backwards to the side of the enclosure. Blazer toppled and Red bore down on him. The white dog was now on his back, Red standing over him, the dog's head moving in and out, Blazer parrying each downward thrust with a snap and butt of his head. The powerful Red closed his fangs over the bridge of Blazer's nose and the steel-like jaws squeezed. Blazer managed to turn his head quick enough to avoid having too much damage inflicted. A clash of teeth could be heard as the dog's fangs met. Red disengaged himself and sought another hold; Blazer was fighting from underneath, and if a dog thinks, then at this point Blazer must have been doing just that. He heaved his body forward pushing Red momentarily off him and with lightning speed was up on his feet, blood from his nose on the floor of the barn. The two dogs again met head on. Blazer turned quickly seizing Red's cheek and pulling hard. Red lowered his head and pushed sideways, both dogs straining against each other.

Sean watched the dogs and glanced at Campbell who was too engrossed in what was going on to see him. He looked across at Brady who was equally caught up in the arena. Sean glanced around. The crowd was totally caught up in the meleé; even the cockerel perched up in the rafters was looking down interestedly at the source of the ominous growls and furor below. Sean grinned and turned his attention to the dogs.

The time ticked away in the arena. Red had managed to break Blazer's hold, the dogs having wrestled and pushed, tearing and biting each other with such fury that the spectators had gone quiet in amazement at such aggression.

Both dogs were fast, both were strong and both had stamina. Both had also suffered by the punishment inflicted on the other. Blazer's nose was raw and his shoulder was badly torn. Red's foreleg was gashed and his cheek had been ripped open. After an hour the pair were still going at it although the pace had slowed considerably and Blazer's coat was now saliva-covered and pink in color. Red was also wet and steam rose from his body as he shook and tore into Blazer. Sean again looked over to Campbell and this time catching his eye, he indicated that he would like to speak to him. Campbell came to him and leaned over the wooden pit side.

"If they keep this up neither of 'em will last. What do you reckon, sir?"

Campbell nodded, "Yer right, Sean. I'll speak to Brady."

Campbell managed with some difficulty to negotiate his way across to Brady."Yes, Mr. Campbell, do you concede defeat?" he asked.

"No, I think if you want to save the dogs, we'd have another think."

Brady looked into the pit.

Red was heaving and panting, his movement no longer cat-like and fast but slow and deliberate, his eyes glazed and staring. Blazer was also breathing with difficulty, the blood from his nose hindering his intake of breath. The floor was covered in blood and white and red hairs stuck to the red substance. Altoll looked across at Brady and Campbell.

"I think they will kill each other."

The spectators began to call out. It had been an aggressive and lively battle, no dog giving any sign of quitting and both dogs equally matched. Altoll went over to the two men.

"All right then," Brady conceded, "we'll give them a minute's rest and then try 'em again; if either of them fail to come across the scratch line, the other dog's the winner, if that's agreeable to you, Mr. Campbell?" Campbell nodded.

"Okay."

Sean and Brady's handler stepped in and took up the dogs and carried them back to their corners. Sean quickly examined Blazer. He had lost a lot of blood and obviously couldn't last much longer if he continued. Brady's dog was in a similar condition. Water was put down for the dogs, both drank for a few seconds before being faced at each other. The

Blazer and Red battle away

dogs were released at the same time and each animal rushed toward the other, Blazer going for Red's throat. The red stood up on his hind legs and Blazer caught the already torn foreleg. Red came down and bit into Blazer's neck.

Altoll beckoned the two handlers once again and the dogs were separated. Campbell handed Sean a blanket he had brought with him and Sean gently wrapped it around Blazer's torn and bleeding body.

The crowd applauded the decision, although all bets were off and it had been decided a draw. The dogs had fought long and hard and both had displayed extreme courage and game spirit.

Brady shook Campbell's hand.

"That's a fine dog you've got there, Campbell. I didn't think he'd match Red."

Campbell commented on the prowess of Red and thanked Brady for the match. Sean carried Blazer out to the buckboard pushing his way through the crowd.

"Are you not going to stay, Mr. Campbell?" Spencer asked as he caught sight of Campbell leaving.

"No thanks, Jim, I would like to get on home. Thanks all the same. Thank Meg for letting me use the front room and tell her she's right; it isn't Christian." Spencer raised his eyebrows, "I'll do that, Mr. Campbell. Goodnight to you."

The buckboard trundled back towards the estate. Blazer lay in the back wrapped in the blanket; the cold night air caused the men's breath to be visible as they spoke.

"Well, he got up a good fight for us," Sean said as he turned round and tucked the blanket around the dog.

"He did that, Sean. That Red is about one of the toughest dogs I've ever seen."

"Well, he wasn't tough enough to beat Blazer, that's for sure. Are you gonna give him another crack at Red?"

"I don't know, Sean. I've been thinking maybe I've had enough of this. Maybe I'll let the dog have a blow."

Sean nodded and looked at Campbell, "Well there's one thing for sure I won't miss and that's these blasted cold nights travelling God knows how many miles."

Campbell agreed, "Anyway we'll see how he is; he ought to be okay in a couple of weeks with a lot of rest and plenty of food."

Chapter 12

The next morning Mrs. Arnot's buckboard turned into the Campbells' drive and pulled up outside the house. Mary jumped off and raced toward the barn.

"Mummy, I'm going to see Blazer. I haven't seen him for ages."

"All right, dear," Mrs. Arnot replied as she climbed down from the buckboard.

"I'll be with Mrs. Campbell."

Mary raced to the barn door and pulled it open. Blazer lifted his head and gave a bark and then wagged his tail feebly. The little girl stood and looked in amazement at the torn and battered warrior. The dog's nose was badly torn, the bridge now swollen, almost closing his eyes, his neck was gashed and he was suffering from muscular stiffness.

"Blazer!" the little girl cried out in dismay.

Mary and Blazer reunited

"Blazer, what happened?" Mary walked slowly toward the dog, tears filled her eyes as she looked at the torn warrior.

"Oh Blazer, you poor thing." She knelt down and gently stroked him on his head wherever he wasn't torn. She pulled the blanket tenderly over the prostrate dog. Blazer gently lay his head back and closed his eyes. Mary quietly left him asleep and still sobbing she turned to run back to the house.

Sean came through the door and Mary collided with him.

"Hey there—steady," Sean said as he steadied the little girl.

"Sean, Sean, Blazer's hurt, he's all cut and hurt," the little girl sobbed and tears rolled down her cheeks.

"Hey, hey, he's all right." The sight of the little girl so upset made him feel guilty at his part in Blazer's condition.

"What happened, Sean? What happened to him?"

Sean didn't know what to say; he could hardly say that nice Mr. Campbell had entered the dog against another in order to win a wager.

"Well he had a scrap with another dog."

Mary looked up at Sean, "A fight? Oh how nasty! I hope he killed the nasty mean dog for hurting him so much."

"Well, he had a damn, I mean, a real good try."

"Will he get better, Sean, will he?"

"Of course he will, he'll be as right as rain in a few weeks. You mark my words."

"Oh can I look after him while he's getting better? Please, Sean, can I?"

"Well, you'll have to be asking Mr. Campbell about that one, Mary."

Mary raced out of the barn and across to the house.

"Now what, Blazer, me old mate. Trouble is with women they always get their own way." Sean crossed over to the dog and gently lifted the dog's head.

"All you need is a jolly good sleep and you'll be on your feet in no time."

Mary burst into the front room where her mother and Fiona Campbell were taking coffee.

"Mary, come and show Aunt Fiona your new dress."

"Aunt Fiona, can I come and look after Blazer? He's sick. Can I please?"

"Of course you can, my dear, and why have you been crying?"

Mary's mother took the little girl's hand.

"Now how can you look after Blazer?"

"I can come every day on Jasper and look after him."

"Well I think you'd better ask Uncle Ian."

At that moment Campbell had come through the door.

"What are you going to ask Uncle Ian?" he said lifting the little girl up and swinging her in the air.

"Blazer's been hurt, hurt bad. He was fighting another dog and got beat up."

"Was he?" Campbell said, surprised at what the little girl had said but convinced that she didn't know the true story.

"Yes, I know, Mary. It was a wild dog he had fought and chased it off. It was worrying my sheep."

Fiona Campbell sighed resignedly and poured Mrs. Arnot another cup of coffee.

"Ian, Janet has invited us to dinner next month. I've said that would be fine."

"Yes, lovely. Thank you, Janet."

Campbell put the little girl down and took a biscuit from one of the plates.

"Now if you'll excuse me, ladies, I have work to do."

Mary approached Campbell. "Can I, Uncle Ian, can I?"

"All right but you must be home by three o'clock in the afternoon."

"Oh thanks," Mary turned and raced out of the house towards the barn, shouting as she ran "Blazer—Blazer I'm going to look after you."

Sean was just leaving as Mary crossed from the house.

"Uncle Ian says it's all right. Sean, I can look after Blazer."

"Well that's just grand," the Irishman said and tousled the little girl's hair, "just grand."

In the following weeks Mary came every day after morning school and sat with Blazer. She wrapped him up and when he was able to walk again she took him slowly around the estate by the pond and reprimanding him if he walked fast.

Campbell watched from the window amused at the little girl scolding the white scarred warrior, the dog looking up at her as if understanding her every word. Sean often walked with little Mary and enjoyed listening to her ideas and the things she was going to do when she grew up.

"I'll be twelve soon, Sean, and soon as I'm eighteen I'm going to England and get married to a rich Englishman."

"Is that so? Well, you could be doing a lot worse. And what about Blazer? Who's going to be looking after him then?"

"Oh, I'll take him with me, that's if Mr. Campbell says it's all right."

Sean laughed. "If he keeps going the way he has been he won't last that long."

"Oh Sean, don't say that," Mary knelt down beside Blazer and put her arms around his tough neck still scarred from the fight. The dog snuffled and butted her gently with his scarred head.

"Come on, Missy, you must be getting back home. Blazer'll be here tomorrow."

That evening Fiona and Ian Campbell drew up outside Tom Arnot's place as arranged for dinner.

Tom was a farmer and didn't believe in standing on ceremony. He spoke his mind and couldn't stand any of that 'sissy nonsense' which Bostonians were noted for: china tea cups and little fingers in the air. On the other hand, he appreciated fine quality and good people and he liked and admired Campbell, even though he disagreed with him as to his habit of dog fighting. In the back of the buckboard sat a familiar figure—the canine shape of a tough old dog.

Arnot came out and greeted the couple.

"Good evening, Fiona, Ian, and I see you've brought him with you."

"Yes Tom, I was thinking about it and you've finally persuaded me to see the error of my ways,"

Blazer and the sleeping Mary

Campbell said good humoredly as he helped his wife down.

"He eats a lot and needs plenty of exercise."

From upstairs a curtain was drawn back and the face of a little girl pressed against the glass. Her eyes lit up and she vanished from the window—a few seconds later to reappear at the door.

"Uncle Ian, Uncle Ian!" She ran up to Campbell and flung her arms around his waist and then over to the white dog who was wagging his tail and barking.

"Blazer, Blazer come on, come on.!" The dog jumped down and waddled after the little girl as she ran inside the house and up the stairs and into her bedroom.

That night just before they left, Fiona and Ian Campbell peeped into Mary's bedroom. The little girl was fast asleep and the only movement was Blazer's right eye as the lid opened momentarily and then with a deep sigh the dog closed it, stretched himself and with the merest quiver of his tail fell back to sleep.